THE PROFESSOR WORE PRUSSIAN BLUE

MYSTERIOUS DEVICES

BOOK SIX

SHELLEY ADINA

Moonshell
Books

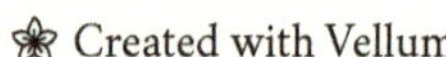 Created with Vellum

PRAISE FOR SHELLEY ADINA

"Shelley Adina adds murder to her steampunk world for a mysteriously delicious brew! You'll love watching her intrepid heroine (and unexpected friends) bring justice to the Wild West while pursuing a quest of her own."

— VICTORIA THOMPSON, BESTSELLING AUTHOR OF *MURDER IN THE BOWERY*

"Shelley Adina has brilliantly combined steampunk with the 'clockwork cozy' in this series in which a young painter solves mysteries. Best of all, the novels feature familiar characters I love from her bestselling Magnificent Devices series. I can't wait for the next book!"

— NANCY WARREN, USA TODAY BESTSELLING AUTHOR

"Prepare to be heartwarmed!"

— LORI ALDEN HOLUTA, LICENSE TO QUILL

*For Emma Jane Holloway and Rachel Goldsworthy
who know a little more than is comfortable about pirates*

THE PROFESSOR WORE PRUSSIAN BLUE

CHAPTER 1

PORT TOWNSEND, THE COLUMBIA TERRITORY

Tuesday, January 14, 1896
8:20 a.m.

ropriety?" Frederica Linden's voice rose in disbelief. "Papa, after all we have been through to find you—facing death at gunpoint, near drowning, to say nothing of keeping ourselves and you out of gaol—your concern now is *propriety?*"

Professor Rudolph Linden gazed at his younger daughter as if still unable to reconcile this outspoken young woman with the shy flower from whom he had been forcibly separated two years before. Daisy could not blame him. But neither could she agree with him.

"Freddie is right, Papa," she said, laying a gentle hand on the Prussian Blue wool of his greatcoat's sleeve. "We are women now, and long past the point of fretting over whether or not society approves of us."

"They cannot help but approve of you," William Barnicott

said softly, "when you helped to prevent a war and the loss of a kingdom only weeks ago."

And here in Port Townsend, had helped to solve not one, but three murders. That had been back in October, and they had been here all this time in spite of their impatience to be on their way, on the final leg of the journey that had begun so long ago. But the circuit judge waited for no man, and when he finally arrived, their testimony had been necessary during the trial.

But there had been sunnier days during the gloomy ones, too. Sunny days of courtship, and laughter, and a realization that a separation they had once taken for granted need not happen at all. Hence their opposition to Papa's old-fashioned concerns.

But he had recovered himself, and straightened his back in a way Daisy remembered well from childhood. "I realize the truth of all you have said. But my dear girls, society in Victoria is unaware of your triumphs and your trials. Your reputation and success depend upon the worthy matrons who rule the dining rooms and ballrooms in which you will appear. And all they will hear is that Frederica Linden arrived, unchaperoned, in the company of an unmarried aeronaut."

They stood on the military airfield on the far side of the hill from Port Townsend, the sea breeze tugging impatiently at skirts and hats, as though urging them to go. The winter sun laid a carpet of glittering sparkles on the water as it rose above the barrier islands. Daisy agreed with the wind—they should have lifted an hour ago, before dawn. Before they attracted notice. And now, practically on the point of departure, Papa was flying the flag of propriety to four individuals who gave not a fig for it.

Five, if one counted Davey, down on the rocks looking for anything interesting the tide might have cast up.

Literally an hour from the end of their journey, who cared if Freddie flew in the Royal Canadian Airborne Police vessel with Corporal Oscar Kent, that dear man, who could be nothing other than a paragon of gentlemanly virtue no matter what he did? He was their escort, for goodness sake.

Well, Freddie cared. How deeply remained to be seen.

"I believe he means to propose, Daisy," she had confided last night, in the sleeping cupboard in the Chemakum long-house, when their farewell celebration on the beach hosted by their friends the Chalmers family had died away to glowing embers and everyone had made their way to bed.

"And do you mean to accept him?" Daisy whispered back, careful to keep her voice down so that the spirits sharing the longhouse with them would not be disturbed.

Freddie had been silent, but Daisy could hear her breath hitch, as though she had tried to reply but had thought better of it. Then her sister said, "Without his help, we might not have recovered Papa, or ended the reign of horrors up there on the cliff."

"Gratitude is, I suppose, one foundation for a marriage," Daisy said solemnly. "But I do not think it wears well in the wash."

"You sound like Lin."

"Do not underestimate the wisdom of our young friend. But if you will not answer me, then I suppose I must remain in suspense indefinitely."

"I—I am almost certain," Freddie faltered. "And one ought to be completely so, oughtn't one? The way you and William are certain."

"We have been through enough danger and joy for two lifetimes," Daisy said by way of agreement. "It has built a solid foundation of trust and love that I am willing to bet my life on, as Davey might say. But you have only known Corporal Kent for three months, and in the beginning at least, you gave every evidence of despising him."

"I did." Freddie turned on to her back and sighed. "Fool that I was. I have been trying to make up for that. And what about my—my ability?"

"It seems to me that he might have an idea about that already, if he was paying attention to our tale of what happened in San Francisco de Assis."

"And I did rather expose myself at the beginning of our acquaintance," Freddie said. "When I asked the spirits' permission for him to enter the camp."

"He will have seen the best of you, then. If he loves you, Freddie, he will accept you as you are. As you must do for him."

"There is a lot of good in him to accept, isn't there?" she said, snuggling down under the beautifully worked quilt. "And I must say, I feel quite a jolt when I see him unexpectedly, as though my heart were struck by a tiny bolt of lightning."

"That is enough to be going on with," Daisy said, snuggling down, too. "If he should propose, and you are still not certain, simply tell him so. Delaying and prevaricating are a poor beginning. Honesty and truth between you are the first necessity, and allows him to go on from there with honor."

Freddie had found her hand and given it a squeeze. "I am glad you are my sister."

Daisy's throat had closed up with love. "It is very much mutual, dearest."

So now, here they stood on the breezy airfield, some of their party very much in favor of Freddie flying aboard the RCAP ship, if it meant the possibility of a very important question.

Daisy supposed she had better collect her young ward before any more time was wasted. "Davey!" she called down to the shore from the edge of the airfield. "What are you doing? Leave those birds alone." The rascal, seeing how close he could get to a flock of sandpipers before they saw him? Did he not know departure was imminent? "Davey!"

When he straightened to look up at her, the entire flock took wing, wheeling up and over the waves. Crestfallen, he climbed up the rocks to where she stood in the grass.

"You scared them," he complained. "I was so close I could almost touch one."

"*You* scared them," she corrected him, ruffling his hair. "And to what purpose? Come. We are in the midst of an argument about propriety and chaperones. It is ridiculous, but Papa will not be moved. Perhaps you can make yourself useful, and throw your weight on our side."

Papa was shaking his head as they joined the little group. "I am afraid I cannot permit it. I can confidently predict that our standing in Victoria society will be in peril enough without adding such a misstep."

"I can go as chaperone, Professor," Davey said cheerfully. "Freddie and I have flown miles together in the conveyance. Avoided them big gunships in the Columbia, too, that sent the *Barbara Carol* so far out to sea we beat you here."

Papa regarded him gravely. "And will you explain all this to the Lieutenant-Governor and his wife when we pay our addresses to them?"

A chink appeared in Davey's cheer, and his gaze faltered. "Lieutenant-Governor?" Daisy knew perfectly well Davey's experience with the authorities did not inspire confidence in his young heart. So much for his persuasions.

"Then I shall go," William said.

"You shall not," Daisy retorted. "You must pilot the conveyance. And I will not be separated from you in any case. Arriving in San Francisco without you was enough for me. I shall not do it again."

"Shall we play musical chairs all the morning?" their father demanded. "No. I shall pilot the conveyance and my daughters will assist me. Davey and William will go with Corporal Kent, and that is an end to it. Come. We do not want to be caught over the islands after midmorning. You know what Mr. Chalmers said."

"We c'n outrun any old pirates," Davey said scornfully. "They won't bother us anyhow. Not with the RCAP vessel as escort—even such a little one as that."

But Papa was not listening. He was loading the traveling closet into the rear of the conveyance and heaving Daisy's and Freddie's valises in after it.

William's and Davey's things were already aboard. Papa climbed into the pilot's chair and asked Davey to stand by at the ropes.

Daisy gritted her teeth and tried not to begin her protests all over again. How had she forgotten about Papa's stubborn streak in all the months they had been pursuing him?

"I guess that decision is made, then." William took Daisy into his arms and kissed the frustrated set of her mouth back into softness while her father was distracted, leaning out of the viewing port on the far side. "We will not be out of sight of one another. I shall spend the whole time anxiously watching your father pilot my contraption, and paying no attention whatever to poor Oscar's engines."

"Papa is an engineer himself, darling," Daisy said, secretly rejoicing at the freedom the ruby on her finger gave her to call him that. "He has already gone over the conveyance with you. Neither of us must worry. You are quite right. You will be within view the whole way."

"You'll make sure he knows that the boiler must be—"

"Yes, I'll go back there myself to be certain."

"And the trim? I forgot to tell him about the trim. Even if there are only three of you—"

"William, if we can pull our friends out of the sea during a ship's capsizing in a heavy swell, his piloting two ladies to a perfectly normal landing field will be easier than drinking tea in Mrs Willamette's drawing room. Much easier, now that I think of it."

William went reluctantly up the RCAP vessel's gangway. Above his head, the fuselage swelled, the RCAP emblem of the fierce osprey's head surrounded by golden maple leaves proudly displayed. On a twisted banner formed by the colors of the Union Jack rode the motto Ius Confirma. Daisy translated it silently: *Uphold the Right.* As if to counter this splendor, the vessel had no name printed upon its bow, only a workmanlike number: 13.

Oh, dear.

She shook off the superstitious unease and tried not to watch as Corporal Kent took Freddie's hand and pressed something into it. With a glance at the conveyance and the steam rising from the boiler's pipes, Freddie shoved it hastily into the pocket of her traveling skirt. She joined Daisy with only a single longing glance back, climbed in, and barely had time to seat herself before Papa called, "Up ship!" as though this were a proper airship and Davey an entire ground crew.

The conveyance tilted until Davey ran around to release the stern rope. Once they were in trim, Daisy climbed into the midsection to manage the boiler. Through the porthole, she saw the corporal's ground crew salute smartly and release the ropes of Number Thirteen. And then she must concentrate on her own task of working the boiler and not imagine William jogging to the stern of the RCAP vessel to manage the engines, nor to wonder if Davey had put a handkerchief in his pocket and tied his boots properly.

Ten minutes later, the boiler was up to full steam, they had reached Papa's chosen altitude, and Daisy was able to take her place on the bench next to Freddie. Below them, the grassy meadows of the peninsula north of Port Townsend extended to the silvery doorstep of the sea. Far below, steamships and sailing vessels threaded their way among the islands of the archipelago. Had anyone below looked up, they would have seen them passing among the clouds, from cool mist to equally cool sunshine and back again.

"It is a pity they must use seagoing vessels," Papa said. "Air travel is so much more efficient."

"It is," Daisy agreed, seeing that Freddie was absorbed in reading the folded square of paper the corporal had given her. "Perhaps they are heavily loaded."

"No, that is not the reason." Papa adjusted the vanes slightly, glancing to starboard at the curve of Number Thirteen's fuselage coming out of a cloud a quarter mile off. "It is the air pirates. Apparently they do not waste their time upon seagoing vessels unless they find no other prey to pursue."

"Who told you such a thing, Papa?" Daisy asked.

"The captain of the *Barbara Carol,* before we berthed in Port Townsend."

Hmph. That coward. Pirates or no, he had scuttled away the moment he could, leaving Daisy in the lurch with no witness to vouch for Papa's whereabouts, and the latter languishing hopelessly in gaol facing charges of murder. She had no great opinion of the man's grasp of facts if he had no grip upon his fears. And if their paths ever crossed, she would tell him so to his face.

"We ought to drop down a hundred feet," Papa said, adjusting the vanes again. "Below these clouds, where visibility is better."

To starboard lay a particularly long island as they made the slight descent. A gust of wind smacked the conveyance and made it sway like a pendulum. "We ought to have started earlier," their father muttered. "Ridiculous delay, arguing over who was flying with whom."

From the corner of her eye, Daisy saw Freddie slide the paper back into her pocket, a dreamy expression in her eyes.

Beyond her sister's profile, through the viewing port, Daisy could see Number Thirteen emerge once more from another cloud. When their escort descended to match their altitude, it was clear its pilot was watching their position with the utmost care.

A shadow slid over the RCAP vessel's fuselage.

Surely the cloud was not moving that fast? Daisy leaned forward to get a better look. Freddie glanced at her, then swung her gaze to starboard, too.

A shape formed within the cloud, then burst from it.

An airship.

Its gondola had been painted gray, its fuselage too—a shade halfway between cloud and sky, and difficult to see even in partly clear weather. The gondola was mounted toward the rear, and under the bow was a second one, mostly isinglass except for the bare minimum of iron supports needed to mount a gun.

No civilized ship outside of the Texican Ranger or RCAP vessels carried mounted guns. Already the gunner was bringing its ugly snout to bear on Number Thirteen.

"Papa!" Daisy exclaimed. "Pirates!"

The gun belched a gout of flame and a projectile was catapulted from it. It pierced the rear quarter of Number Thirteen from one longitudinal strut to the other, and the rear third of the fuselage collapsed.

"Oscar!" Freddie shrieked.

"William! Davey!" Daisy cried as she slid over to Freddie's side, her horrified gaze locked on the distressed vessel.

The conveyance tilted. Papa gave a shout and flung out a hand to snatch at Daisy's sleeve. "Get back!" he commanded. "You will throw off our trim." He dragged her back with surprising strength.

"No!" she moaned. "Oh, no!"

For the RCAP vessel could not recover. With another shot from the pirate gun, the center gasbag was pierced, too. Even from here, they could hear a scream like that of an osprey— the lifting gas escaping, tearing a great rip in the gas bag and sending the gondola into a steep dive.

Or maybe it wasn't the lifting gas.

Maybe it was simply their own screams as the doomed ship fell out of the sky toward the unforgiving sea.

CHAPTER 2

*D*aisy's eyes were so full of tears she could barely make out her father, his hands white-knuckled on the navigation wheel and vane levers.

They had not changed their course by so much as a single degree.

"Papa!" She clutched his shoulder and shook it. "Come about. We must rescue them!"

"No."

"No?" she shrieked. "Come about at once. Your future son-in-law has just gone down, and we do not know if he is dead or alive."

"I am aware of the facts, Margrethe."

He never called her Margrethe unless he was on the last shreds of his self-control.

"But Papa—" Freddie began. Her face was as white as any cloud, her gray eyes huge.

"Daisy, get to the boiler and bring her back to full steam. We must reach Victoria with all possible speed."

"Victoria!" both his daughters repeated in disbelief.

"Immediately!"

Daisy flung herself into the boiler compartment and opened up the engine to full, dumping coal into the hopper like a madwoman and wishing that of all things, she had a rocket rucksack so that she might leap from the platform in the rear and go to William's aid.

For it was abundantly clear that their father, along with suffering a loss of memory, had also sustained damage to his brain that affected him in more terrifying ways. They were going to have to remove him from the controls. But he outweighed them both by a considerable margin. Could she sneak up on him with the coal scuttle and—oh, dear heaven.

Of course she could not strike her father, even for William. Who had gone mad now?

"Papa, please," Freddie begged, her voice cracking with tears. "You must turn back. *Please.*"

"It is clear that you girls are under the influence of emotion and not logic," Papa said grimly. They were clear of the peninsula, and out over the open water of the strait between the mainland and Victoria. "We are much closer to Victoria now than the RCAP detachment in Port Townsend. We will report the attack at once, and return within the hour with a full contingent of aeronauts. And until then, you will cease your weeping, do your duty, and for the love of heaven, help me spot the airfield."

If it had not been for the crack in his voice, Daisy's love for her father might have turned to implacable, unforgiving hatred in that moment. But that break, that moment of emotion, told her that he was every bit as concerned for William and Davey as she was. That he had run through every possible scenario in that frighteningly intelligent, slowly recovering brain of his, in only a few seconds, and had arrived at the most effective solution.

She clutched Freddie's hand. "Papa is right, dearest. We need help, and quickly. If we were to turn back, we would most certainly be shot down as well—and do not forget, this vessel is carrying the Viceroy's gold ingot. We must not deliver to those miscreants the reward for our own deaths."

"I have not forgotten," Freddie said hoarsely, hanging on to Daisy's hand as though without it, she might leap out of the viewing port into the sea and swim for shore herself. "But I would surrender it in an instant if it meant our friends' lives."

"As would I," Daisy assured her. "Papa, the engine is at full steam. You may fly as fast as you dare and it will not be fast enough for us."

Within fifteen minutes, they began the most reckless approach Daisy had ever endured. She and Freddie strained their eyes ahead. Where was the airfield? Where would they find the RCAP? How soon could they mount a rescue?

And most pressing of all, had William, Davey, and Corporal Kent survived what must surely have been a crash landing?

As though he had divined her thoughts, Papa said, "My dear, forgive my language a moment ago. You must know that if they survived the crash, your fiancé and the corporal are two of the most capable men in the Columbia Territory. No cowardly air pirate will be able to get the best of them, you may be assured of that."

"I know, Papa." Daisy gripped his shoulder, this time as one might share a burden with another, in mutual sympathy and gratitude. "And there is nothing to forgive."

"There!" Freddie exclaimed, pointing. "The landing field, to the east of the harbor."

The conveyance came in on a short, fast approach. So short and so fast that they were nearly elbowed out of the sky when a graceful ship lifted practically under their noses. It was only thanks to the nimble work of Papa's hands and feet on the controls that they did not collide with the vessel.

"Why, it is *Swan!*" Daisy exclaimed, gawking over her shoulder as Papa brought the conveyance in on a sickening spiral toward an empty space between two larger vessels. "Freddie, look, there is Lady Hollys at the helm."

The much larger airship, silver and blue and swift, fell up into the sky and out of their sight beyond their own buff-and-scarlet balloon.

"She did not see us," Freddie said in frustration. "Otherwise we could have flagged them back, and begged for their help."

"This is not a private matter," Papa said, releasing his harness. "We must appeal to the RCAP to save their own. To the mooring irons, girls, if you please, with all speed."

When the conveyance was moored and their papers inspected, Papa lost no time in asking the field master the location of the headquarters of the Royal Canadian Airborne Police.

"An RCAP vessel was just shot down over the archipelago," Papa said, "with a corporal and our friends aboard. We must mount a rescue without delay."

The field master pushed her goggles back on top of her cap, her gaze a mixture of horror and sympathy. "I'll send a tube. By the time someone receives it, they'll be ready for you. You'll want to go straight to the Birdcages." She pulled over a blank square of message paper. Quickly, she sketched the route, ending at a sketch of several rounded edifices that looked enough like the Brighton Pavilion to bring a puzzled frown to Daisy's forehead.

"The Birdcages?" she repeated.

"A nickname. It is where the government of the territory is housed like so many ravens and argumentative blue jays." The field master filled in street names in clear, efficient capitals. "The barracks is to the rear, here. The entire wing." She handed them the map. "You will find a landau for hire at the north end of the field. After I dispatch the tube, I will send pigeons, advising incoming vessels to be on their guard if Pig Iron Kelly is back on the prowl."

Pig Iron Kelly. Was that who commanded the air pirates? Daisy would have no trouble remembering *that*.

As they left the sturdy little shed, they heard the pneumatic *swoosh* of a tube being sucked into the mail system. Outside of the installation at the Bonnell home, this was the first they had seen on this continent. The Canadas, of which the Columbia Territory was a part, appeared to enjoy a slight advantage in the field of technology over the Texican Territories to the south. For some reason, she found this comforting. Familiar. And every small advantage was sure to help.

The hired landau conveyed them to the Birdcages by what appeared to be the most efficient route on the field master's map. Daisy paid the pilot and they hurried up the drive to the barracks at the back of the most imposing yet fanciful set of government buildings she had ever laid eyes on.

"Who on earth approved the plans for this?" she heard her father mutter. "It looks like a set of those crinolines your grandmother used to wear."

"I think they're pretty." Freddie seemed determined to find a bright spot anywhere she could.

Two sergeants at arms greeted them as they rushed into the marble-floored foyer of the headquarters. "State your business," one of them said, standing straight as a pike, his hands clasped behind his back. Like Corporal Kent, both wore the aeronaut's cap and goggles. Unlike him, there was only one gold chevron stitched on the shoulders of their khaki sleeves, not two.

Papa nodded briefly in greeting. "We have been attacked," he said without preamble. "Our conveyance was being escorted here by Corporal Oscar Kent of your company in an RCAP vessel."

"Number thirteen," Daisy put in, trying to be helpful. "Two members of our party accompanied him."

"A grey ship bearing a mounted gun and manned by pirates shot the RCAP vessel down over the archipelago," Papa went on. "We beg you to help us recover Corporal Kent and our friends, and bring these miscreants to justice."

The second constable had already disappeared up the stairs. The first one nodded. "Pig Iron Kelly, may his soul be da— er, I beg your pardon, ladies. Consigned to perdition. Come with me."

This was the most hospitable welcome Daisy had received from any policing force since their long journey had begun. She dared to feel a little hope that help might actually be forthcoming, and no one would be tossed out—or clapped in gaol.

They were shown into an office not unlike the one Oscar Kent had occupied in Port Townsend, only larger and with finer woods used in its construction. A man who rather resembled the osprey in the RCAP crest rose as they entered, the other constable standing at attention beside the door. The older officer's eyes were dark and piercing, his nose imposing, and while his head was bare, the hair at his temples was going gray in wings combed back in an attempt at control. In the shape of his jaw and the arch of his brows, Daisy recognized someone almost familiar.

Freddie drew in a breath as her gaze fell upon an engraved pen stand upon the desk. Fortunately, they both had become quite good at reading upside down.

PRESENTED TO INSPECTOR MARCUS I. KENT
IN RECOGNITION OF TWENTY YEARS OF MERITORIOUS SERVICE
TO HER MAJESTY AND THE ROYAL CANADIAN AIRBORNE POLICE

"You are Oscar's father," Freddie said on a note of wonder, and quite without benefit of introduction or invitation.

The inspector's brows rose as he waved them into chairs before the desk. "I am. And you are?"

"Well, I might have been his fiancée by now, if my father had permitted me to fly with him this morning."

Daisy felt almost faint at the enormity of this breach of civility, to say nothing of its disrespect to Papa. Only the most dire extremes of fear and anxiety within a woman's heart could produce such brutal frankness.

But Inspector Kent did not even flinch. He merely seated himself. "Then you would have been shot down, too, and your family blessedly unaware of what happens to women once they are in the clutches of Pig Iron Kelly."

Freddie's brief foray into forthrightness collapsed as surely as the fuselage of Number Thirteen. "What ... happens?"

"I will not assault your ears with the details, young lady, but suffice it to say that if a woman should survive, she no longer has the courage to fight, or leave, or even save herself. Now, let us abandon speculation and proceed to facts. You know who I am. May I ask once again who you are?"

"I am Frederica Linden." Freddie was clearly trying to bear up under the horrors this recitation had provoked. "This is my sister Daisy, and our father, Professor Rudolph Linden."

A most peculiar expression was forming on the inspector's face. The constables exchanged a glance between themselves.

"The Lindens, you say." He took them in, one after the other. "I saw the report of the murder of Judge Wilson Bonnell in Port Townsend. You are the family the superintendent wrote of. Who solved the murder."

"We are," Daisy said.

"At one time, Wilson Bonnell was one of my closest friends," Inspector Kent said gruffly. "For finding his killer and seeing justice done, you have my gratitude." His gaze moved to Papa, as though considering how close the latter had come to being hanged in the place of that same killer. "And now you come with a report of a different kind, for which I must be grateful as well. For if you had not witnessed this cowardly attack, I might never have known of Corporal Kent's fate until some bit of the ship's fuselage washed up near enough to a detachment to be identified."

"We must form a rescue party at once," Papa said. "Every ship you can muster. We must overcome the enemy and recover your son, my elder daughter's fiancé, and her young ward."

The inspector's jaw hardened and a flicker of grief passed

over his face, like the distant lightning presaging a storm. "I can spare two ships."

"Two?" Papa's beard practically stiffened with affront. "There are only two ships to spare in the capital and Port Townsend combined? How can that be?"

"Have you not seen a newspaper?" Inspector Kent asked with careful politeness that concealed no sarcasm.

Papa and his daughters exchanged a mystified glance. "Not in weeks."

One of the constables cleared his throat. "It's the royal visit, Professor. Her Majesty's grandson, the Duke of Cornwall, has been proceeding west from Charlottetown with his wife all last week."

"Yes, yes, a lot of foufarrah and nonsense," Inspector Kent snapped. "The devil of it is that the RCAP is taking the escort of Their Royal Highnesses in relays. Six of our ships have just departed—three from here and three from Port Townsend."

"Along with that of Captain Sir Ian and Lady Hollys," the second constable added. "They just lifted."

"Yes, we saw them. They nearly collided with us," Daisy said. "But never mind. We will happily accept the assistance of two ships and as many aeronauts as you can spare. When can we lift?"

The inspector eyed her. "*We* will do no such thing. My men will lift when they are prepared. Within the hour, I hope. *You* will stay here, safely out of reach."

"Stay here—but William—!"

"And Oscar—we must go!" Daisy and Freddie both spoke at once.

"You will not, and if you try, I will impound the vessel you came in. Am I perfectly clear?"

Daisy could not breathe. It had never once occurred to her that they would not go to the aid of those they loved. It was unthinkable.

Impossible. They must find a way.

Inspector Kent rose to indicate the briefing was over. "I know what you are thinking. Be assured that I am thinking the same. The life of Corporal Kent is every bit as important to me as it is to you." He gazed at Freddie, and she straightened her spine to gaze back. Daisy was rather reminded of a robin facing down a much larger raptor.

But she could not deny that the raptor was far better fitted to seek and find its prey. It had resources to command that the robin did not. And for that, Daisy could only be grateful.

"Oscar's father is right, dearest," she murmured, taking Freddie's cold hand in her own. "Love will see him safe, you'll see."

Freddie's mouth trembled. "Do you promise?"

But her gaze lay upon the inspector, who firmed his jaw and did not reply.

CHAPTER 3

WHITBY ISLAND

9:30 a.m.

When he had ascertained that he was not in fact dead, and could breathe, William unclipped his safety harness and located Davey. The boy was wrapped around a pipe like a boa constrictor, having disobeyed a direct order from his captain about the necessity of the harness and lived to learn his lesson.

"Are you all right?"

"Aye," the boy said as though he couldn't quite believe it. "I don't think we should move about much, though."

William didn't, either. The gondola was pointed at a steep angle directly down the side of a cliff at least a hundred feet high. The rest of the collapsed fuselage, caught in the thick branches of the pines and cedars to the stern, appeared to be all that was keeping them from plunging headlong into the sea.

"Corporal?" William watched as their erstwhile captain attempted to find his footing among a landslide of charts, instruments, and the upended navigation table, which had all landed in the bow and were now partially blocking the unsavory view of the restless, heaving waves. "I trust you have suffered no injuries?"

"None that matter," Corporal Kent said briefly. "Did you see whether the Lindens got away?"

"They did," Davey reported, rather as though he hoped good news would mitigate his disobedience. "Question is, where's that pirate ship?"

"Not far away, you may be certain." The corporal swung himself to the aft hatch on his safety line, and shoved on it. It opened to reveal an expanse of sheer rock and, above their heads, the edge of the cliff. A raven standing on an overhanging tree branch tilted its head to inspect them, its black eyes glinting. "Come. We must get away before we are captured."

"What'll they do to us?" Davey slid to what had been the stairs up to the cabins, and swung down to cling to William as though the latter had been a pipe, too.

"They will shoot me, I expect, holding me to blame for Pig Iron Kelly's taking a bullet to the leg recently during a skirmish. But you? They will likely hold you for ransom."

"Ransom from whom?" William gripped Davey with one arm and, using his safety line, swung across the chaos to the door. "We could simply say we are lone travelers."

"They will amuse themselves with you until they get a name," the corporal said with chilling brevity. "If you hold out, they will offer you a place among their number. If you refuse, you will be shot."

"Friendly lot," Davey said faintly.

"It is best that we are not captured." He unclipped his line and climbed out on the top of the gondola on hands and knees.

"We must hold out until Daisy raises the alarm and the RCAP come to our rescue," William said with as much good cheer as he could muster.

"I was a fool not to have taken a civilian ship," the corporal muttered. "I lost my good sense in favor of seeing Frederica safely to Victoria in respectable style."

"Well, you did that," Davey pointed out. "They'll have got there by now."

William pushed him out the door, where he scrambled to join the captain.

"Yes, but I had hoped to disembark with her. Make myself useful to her family. Take in the sights and escort her to balls and assemblies."

"In other words, a proper courtship that did not include long hours in the witness's chair." William unclipped his own line and hauling himself out into the windy morning. Above, the rigging lines were taut, their lengths caught in the trees, while the remaining third of the fuselage did its best to remain buoyant under the dead weight of the unbalanced gondola. It would not remain so for much longer.

"Yes." Corporal Kent pressed a hand to the inside pocket of his uniform jacket, over his heart. "At least this is still safe."

"What is?" Davey could always be counted on to ask questions, whether the occasion called for them or not.

"My mother's diamond engagement ring. I am very glad it is on my person, and not somewhere in the bow under a layer of debris. Come, enough talk. Davey, do you think you can make it to safety if I throw you?"

The grassy verge of the cliff edge was no more than ten

feet from where they balanced on the top of the gondola. Ten impossible feet, in William's opinion.

"No," Davey said.

"None of us can jump so far," William said.

"One of us must," Corporal Kent said, "and fasten one of these lines to something solid so that the others may cross."

"We'd do better to go back into the bow and jump out the viewing port into the sea," Davey observed. William couldn't fault his logic.

"And the cold water would put an end to your body's ability to move. Even if you could find a beach on which to get out among these cliffs, you could not run and evade capture afterward," Corporal Kent told him. "In the winter, these waters are cold enough to squeeze the breath and heat from your body."

"We must climb the ropes," William decided. "Into the trees, and climb down from there."

Of their three options, it was the least likely to conclude with bodies washing up on a beach somewhere in the archipelago.

Davey went first—only because he shinnied up a rigging line and was out of reach before anyone could stop him. William watched, hardly able to breathe, as he crossed the pounding void beneath, then up the taut line, slower now, until he could swing himself from it into the branches of a straight, thick fir tree.

A tree that appeared to be naked of branches for at least forty feet above the ground, and too thick around to be encompassed by a man's limbs. William was uncomfortably reminded of the pinnacle cells in Santa Fe. And here they were without so much as a ruffled petticoat with which to save themselves as Daisy and Freddie had done.

"Of all the luck," the corporal groaned. "The Douglas firs grow like that. Why couldn't there have been an arbutus or an oak at hand?"

But Davey was not merely sitting like a bird on a branch, waiting to be rescued. He was not that sort of boy. Instead, he had managed to reach one of the thick mooring lines hanging down from the ruined fuselage and wrestled it over a branch as thick as his own body. He hauled it up, wrapped it once more around the branch, then let it fall.

Then, as easily as any sailor, he wrapped his legs around the rope and used his boots to adjust his speed as he slid down it to the ground.

"Well, I'll be a spiky urchin," Corporal Kent said blankly.

"Davey Fletcher is a very useful and resourceful young man," William said proudly. "After you, Corporal."

"Indeed not. Civilians first. And do for heaven's sake call me Oscar. We cannot simultaneously observe rank and be marooned on a pirate-infested island."

Time was of the essence, so William did not argue. "Then you must call me William."

He launched himself along the rope, and ten rather terrifying minutes later, found himself on the ground next to Davey, his hands burning from the rope and his gaze pinned on Oscar, who had nearly reached the Douglas fir.

With a groan, the gondola tilted further as some of the collapsed fuselage broke the branches under it and gave way. The line sagged and Oscar's feet lost their grip. He hung there, swinging from the rope with both hands, forty feet in the air.

Forward. Back.

He used his legs like a gymnast and on the apex of the next arc, let go of the rope and sailed six or seven feet into the arms of the fir.

"Topping," Davey said with admiration.

Within a few minutes, the corporal had joined them on the ground, a little pale under his tan and three inches of the left sleeve of his jacket pulled out of its shoulder seam.

"Glad you could join us," William said.

"You're not the only one." Oscar dusted off his navy uniform trousers and adjusted the goggles upon his cap. "Let us go, quickly. They'll have spotted where we went down and that fuselage is nothing if not noticeable."

"If help is coming from the north, we ought to head that way," William suggested.

"No, indeed." Oscar had taken the lead position. "Victoria is due southwest. This island is bisected by a deep sound, and we have been unlucky enough to land on the north-eastern side. To reach the side from which our rescuers might come, we must go all the way around the sound and down the far side—a journey that will take two days at least on foot."

"We could build a raft to cross," Davey suggested.

"With what?" Oscar asked him. "We did not come away with Number Thirteen's toolbox."

"Or any food, for that matter," William added.

"I have some chocolate in my pocket," Davey said. He pulled out an unidentifiable lump. "It's a bit melted."

"Save it for later, when we will appreciate it more," Oscar told him.

"We might cut some of the canvas from the fuselage, Oscar, if we are to sleep rough for a night or more," William suggested, eyeing the length of it in the trees overhead, some of it dragging on the ground.

"We must travel light, and be willing to hide in caves and trees," the aeronaut said. "But nights are cold, and wet as well. I have one of Mr. Bowie's knives in my belt. If I cut lengths twice the size of a man, each may wrap up to sleep, or use it for a poncho."

He worked quickly to cut squares of treated flight canvas, which was tough but light. William held the lengths of it steady and told Davey over his shoulder, "I have a Colt revolver like Freddie's, a six-shooter, if need be." His jacket hiked up, showing the weapon in its holster.

"For six pirates?" Davey said hopefully.

"You have a lot of faith in my aim," William said with a smile. "Our Daisy can outshoot me any day."

"There are many more than six pirates," Oscar told them, handing Davey the last, smaller square. "Roll this up. No, we will gather food quietly—shellfish and mushrooms and the like. Come. We must keep out of sight from above. And stay alert."

Victoria

11:25 a.m.

Daisy could barely swallow.

With brisk civility, Inspector Kent had seen her, Freddie and their father seated in the mess hall and had ordered a nourishing lunch. But delicious though the meaty stew and thick slices of freshly baked bread covered in melted cheese were, it was all she could do to get them down. Fear for William and Davey and Oscar had tightened her stomach into what she envisioned as a screw of paper, fit only for lighting fires.

However, one could not appear ungrateful. Besides, she had learned long ago to take advantage of meals when they were offered, since there would inevitably be hunger along the way later. So she nudged Freddie and tilted her head toward her sister's steaming bowl. Freddie nodded, evidently remembering the same lessons, and addressed herself to her meal.

Papa had already finished his, and a uniformed constable obligingly took it away to be refilled.

Word of their errand had evidently spread through the barracks with the speed of a wildfire, for while many of the aeronauts were away on patrol or on royal escort duty, there were still enough left to fill some of the tables near them, or to peer in the doors to see the young lady being courted by Oscar Kent, and the other whose fiancé had gone down in Kent's ship.

By the time the Lindens had finished their lunch, the two RCAP vessels in service at headquarters reported that they were prepared for lift.

"Professor Linden," Inspector Kent said as he approached their table. "If you and your daughters will join me at the briefing, I believe you can offer details that will help my men locate Number Thirteen."

Daisy half thought the inspector might offer his arm to Freddie, but he did not. She supposed that until matters were settled between her sister and the corporal, Inspector Kent would treat them with the same civility with which he appeared to treat everyone.

They hurried outside after him to the ships, where a

contingent of aeronauts presented themselves for inspection and briefing, lining up between the gondolas. Inspector Kent paced between them, examining pistols and equipment, while Daisy craned her neck to see the vessels' names. Number Nineteen. And Number Seven.

Oh, William, be safe. Be clever, and come back to me with Davey running ahead of you to throw himself into my arms.

She must not fall into the pit of despair. The RCAP would not allow their commander's son to be captured and killed, nor the people with him. They would be saved. They would, if all went well, be here by dinner time.

One of the navigators had unrolled a chart, and Inspector Kent waved the Lindens over. "If you would pinpoint the trajectory by which you saw the ship going down," he said, "my men will have a general idea of where to start their search."

Since Papa had been focused on piloting the conveyance out of danger, it fell to Daisy and Freddie to offer what they had seen. "It was this long island," Daisy said, pointing to the one on the map. "Their descent was from here to here." Her finger swept its shape. "We did not see the exact landing, having passed it by then, but given the speed of their fall and Corporal Kent's skill as a pilot, I am sure they would not have overshot the island and landed in the sea."

The two navigators nodded briskly, and one rolled up the chart. "Whitby Island."

"We'll come in from the northeast, then, sir," the other said. "Less danger from the guns, and open water to maneuver if necessary."

"Permission to lift?" the first asked.

Inspector Kent nodded. "Fair winds. And good hunting."

Whitby Island
11:50 a.m.

William might have fooled himself into believing they were out on a pleasant walk, had there not been a sheer cliff on one side and nearly impenetrable rain forest on the other. There was no such thing as level ground, with a thousand years of fallen trees, humps of brambles, and a thick understory, where smaller trees struggled to grow among those that stretched up to the sun.

He glanced up in an attempt to judge its meridian. "Noon?"

The corporal had a chronometer in a pouch on his belt. "Nearly. Four hours of good daylight left, and then we shall have to hope the shore is accessible enough to scavenge the rocks for food."

"What kind of food?" Davey wanted to know, but Oscar did not reply.

For which William was rather grateful.

Oscar pushed through the next thicket and held it for Davey, who asked, "Why don't you cut that down?"

"Because three men already leave a trail for a tracker with mediocre skills," Oscar said. "If I begin dulling my knife on brush, even a rank beginner could follow us. We must be like the deer, slipping unseen among the trees."

William looked down at the great green cushion of moss his booted foot had just torn from a stone. He bent and put it back.

They kept the cliffs on their left, but traveled within the trees so that any vessel not carrying the RCAP emblem would be unable to spot them. William did not know whether to keep a weather eye on the treetops, or on his own path. However, the last thing they needed was a man with a broken leg or a sprained ankle. Best to keep his eyes on the ground and his ears open for the sound of a propeller or a steam engine, both of which would easily be heard passing overhead.

Davey was the most resilient person William knew, but even he was flagging after another hour of climbing and hiking. And then the clouds moved in and the rain began in earnest. William blessed the instincts that had prompted him to suggest they cut the fuselage, for when the squares were tented over them from head to foot, the rain sheeted off them and kept them relatively dry. He made sure that Davey was positioned between himself and Oscar in the lead so that he did not fall behind and become lost in the misty murk.

What would happen if the RCAP were to attempt a rescue? They would be forced to fly low over the treetops and be spotted by the pirates for certain—or above the clouds, and be useless.

But that, he concluded grimly, was not his nevermind. Staying at large and undamaged was, so he must do that with all his might.

Another age of struggling through soaked undergrowth and it seemed that they were descending closer to the sea. Oscar risked a reconnaissance out to the cliff edge, where they saw a rocky beach perhaps a quarter of a mile ahead.

The corporal heaved a grateful sigh. "I had begun to wonder what to do if we could not get down. And we are in luck—the tide is going out."

"How can you tell?" Davey wanted to know. "And why is that lucky?"

"See that line of seaweed along the rocks?" Oscar pointed. "That is high tide. It is above several feet of wet rocks. Too wet to have dried, which means the tide is ebbing. If the rocks were dry, it would be flowing."

"It's raining," Davey pointed out. "All the rocks are wet."

"True enough, but you will find I am right. And it is lucky because the oysters and mussels for our dinner will be exposed. If it were summer, we might dive for them, but not in January."

"How will we cook them?" Davey wanted to know, his voice hollow under the shelter of his canvas.

But again, Oscar did not reply, and William began to suspect this was because neither of them would like the answer.

The sight of the rocky little beach seemed to give them all fresh willingness to press on. Within a few minutes, it seemed, they were making their cautious way down to the water line, eyes darting from sky to sea so they would not be taken by surprise.

"Should we spot a ship when we are out in the open like this," Oscar said in the shelter of a chunk of granite the size of a steam wagon, "take shelter near this rock if you can. Even if you are out in the open, fold yourselves as close to the ground as possible and hide beneath your canvas so that from above, you look like a rock, too."

"Will that really work?" Davey asked.

"I do not know." Oscar smiled, though his eyes were worried. "But it is better than leaping about in a panic and confirming that we are the quarry they seek."

"I have gathered shellfish before," William said. "Clams. On Cape Cod. Not quite the same. What are we looking for?"

"Oysters and mussels will be clinging to these rocks," Oscar told them. "Winkles, too. All of which I have eaten raw on training exercises."

Davey left off his exploration of the foot of the granite boulder. "Raw?"

Oscar nodded. "It is too wet to build a fire. We have no tinder. And even if we found enough wood to use, we run the risk of the smoke being seen above the trees."

"Oysters are quite good raw," William said, trying for a cheerful tone even though his own stomach was quailing at the thought. "One pays a fortune for them in New York."

"I'm not eating raw anything," Davey said from under his canvas while the rain pattered on all of their covered heads. "I'll eat my chocolate."

"Suit yourself," Oscar said. "But when you faint from lack of proper nourishment, we cannot carry you. I suppose, though, that in the event you regain consciousness and you have not been captured, you might crawl out into the open. It's possible we may spot you after we have been rescued."

Davey set his teeth and William distinctly heard a growl.

Or perhaps it was merely the boy's stomach.

Moving slowly, they fanned out upon the rocks, keeping low, and conscious every moment of movement in the skies. Eagles, ospreys, geese, gulls—every one gave William a start. Davey could not bring himself to wrench the unwilling shell-fish off their rocks, so he offered a length of his canvas as a kind of sling between his hands in which to collect them. They did not harvest more than they needed—only a few creatures each. Then they retreated back beneath the trees and hunkered down in the half-shelter of a fallen log whose trunk was taller than Davey.

Oscar shucked the oysters and demonstrated the slide-and-slurp method of consuming them. "Do not let them linger upon the palate," he said. "Our goal is sustenance, not pleasure."

With relief, William saw that Davey had weighed oysters versus being left behind, and chosen the former. At least they had something that would fill their stomachs, even if the thought of the same for breakfast was off-putting in the extreme.

"Perhaps a fire will be possible next time," he croaked.

"Perhaps," Oscar said amiably. "Or perhaps by this time tomorrow, we will be safe in the RCAP barracks, sitting down to a dinner of roast beef and Yorkshire pudding."

"From your lips to God's ears," Davey muttered into his canvas, and knocked back the last of his share.

CHAPTER 4

WHITBY ISLAND

3:15 p.m.

They had just buried the signs of their repast under a thick carpet of leaf mast and fir needles when Davey lifted his head, listening intently. "An engine," he said, and pointed. "Coming from that direction."

Northeast. A bright flame of hope lit in William's chest.

"An engine on whose ship?" Oscar said quietly. "Do we expose ourselves and prepare for rescue, or conceal ourselves and hope our enemy misses us?"

And then the question was answered as the purring sound grew louder, and within moments they could hear the propellers and even the wind singing in the ropes. A medium-sized khaki-colored vessel with the RCAP's fierce osprey on the side passed overhead. A sound was torn from William's throat, half shout, half prayer.

"They have spotted our downed vessel," Oscar said after a moment, as the pitch of the engine changed. "They are coming about."

And then a second engine could be heard, approaching swiftly from the same direction. Pursuer? Or companion ship?

William could hardly breathe from excitement as he craned his neck to look up among the treetops for the first glimpse of a fuselage. And then, to his vast relief, a second RCAP ship passed over them, on the same heading as the first.

"We should've stayed with the wreckage," Davey groaned. "Then they could've picked us up on that headland and made our escape before the pirates even knew we were there."

"We weren't to know that rescue would come so quickly," Oscar told him. "I was fully prepared to sleep rough tonight. It is clear that the Lindens reached Victoria and received assistance far more quickly than I expected." He looked away, an expression in his eyes that William could not read.

"For which we can only be grateful," he said. "The question is, how can we best assist ourselves in our own rescue when we are too far away to run back?"

Oscar's gaze took in the forest around them. "Davey must go up a tree and flag them with his canvas."

"Topping!" Davey's eyes lit up and he began at once to examine likely trees.

"But you must be careful," Oscar said. "Don't—"

"Of course I won't fall," Davey retorted scornfully. "What about that one? It's skinny enough that I can get my legs around it, but it's tall."

"I wasn't going to say *fall*," the corporal said. "I meant you must look carefully about you once you're up there, to make sure there are no pirates before you draw such attention."

"Oh," the boy said. "I would have done that without your telling me. I don't want to get shot out of a tree."

"I don't want that, either," William told him. "Daisy would never forgive me. Off you go, before they pass."

Davey rolled up his wet canvas as tightly as he could and stuffed it down the back of his trousers. Then he shinnied up the tree for several feet before the remains of broken branches gave him footholds, making his progress much faster.

"That boy is proof that the prime minister's father was right," Oscar said. "He, at least, is obviously descended from some sort of monkey."

William had never bothered to wonder if the elder Mr Darwin's hypotheses were right or not. He was just grateful that Davey's skills were now employed in the service of people who loved him, and not by the criminal element of Georgetown, which might likely have been his fate had he not stowed away on the conveyance that cold morning.

Davey disappeared into the top of the fir, his movements concealed by the thick needles and numerous branches. The trunk creaked and appeared to sway a little, though there was no wind.

"He is signaling them," William said. "The coast must be clear."

"The rain is slacking off, too. There is more light to the west. Let us hope—" But Oscar never finished his sentence.

For the light was blocked so thoroughly it was as though twilight had crashed down in a moment. William spun to look through the trunks of the trees between them, where their descent to the shore was just visible, and where the sky was plainly visible. The sight he had been dreading seemed to fill the spaces between the treetops—an expanse of unmarked gray fuselage—a gondola painted the same color. One, two, three ships. A flotilla of deadly ghosts sailing silently on the wind, stalking the two rescue ships who might not yet have detected their presence.

"Pirates!" he exclaimed.

Oscar spun and took in the dreadful sight. "Davey!" he shouted. "Get down!"

The bark of a distant cannon was followed immediately by the crash of a projectile tearing through the trees. Branches flew off treetops, wood splintered with a series of agonized screeches, and the ball crashed to the ground a hundred yards away with a thump that William could feel through his boots.

"Davey!" he shouted, his entire body cold with terror for the boy. There was no reply, and in the shock of the careless shot, William lost track of which tree Davey had climbed. "We've got to go get him. He could be injured."

"At once," Oscar agreed. "And if they send out a ground party, we will be safer in the trees. Take your canvas. We may need them to carry his—"

"If it rains again," William snapped.

This was no time for pessimism. Even if he had been hit by flying wood, Davey was probably clinging to a branch, thanking his lucky stars that the ball itself had missed him. Afraid to move or breathe, of course he would not have returned William's shout.

Oscar, fortunately, could tell one fir from another, and having stowed his canvas, began to climb. William rolled up his own canvas, stuffed it down his trousers, and followed, working around to the opposite side so that bits of bark and moss would not cascade upon his head and scratch their way down into his shirt. Their climb was accompanied by the boom of the pirate guns, and the slightly higher pitch of the

RCAP gunner's return fire. Poor Number Thirteen had been armed, too, but the attack from above, like the stooping of a hawk upon its prey, had left them no time to respond or even to take evasive action.

And then they were in the thick boughs at the top of the tree. "Davey!" he called. "Are you all right?"

"Aye," came a thready voice. "It missed me by inches. That gunner is no slouch."

That did not bode well. If the pirate gunner could nearly pick off a small boy in a treetop, waving a bit of canvas, what could he do with a ship in full flight?

No. This was no time for such thoughts.

William reached Davey, feeling the tree sway under their combined weight. "You're sure you are unharmed?"

"Aye." Davey sat with his back against the thinning trunk, both legs wrapped around a branch, both hands clinging to one just above his shoulder. William came as close as he dared, wondering if the tree could bear them all without snapping. "Look. Three against two. It ent a fair fight at all."

William got his arm around a thick branch and turned his body to gaze out over the forest at the battle in the skies.

"Number Seven," came a hollow voice from the other side of the trunk. Oscar leaned out as far as he dared in order to see. "Two light bow guns and big Daimler engines. Not as much firepower, but fast. And Nineteen. Mounted guns in the bow and a Gatling off the stern, so that's something. Pig Iron Kelly will not get by them so easily. That is his flagship, there. The largest."

Flocks of gulls and ravens were fleeing the skies, beating their way toward other islands where the clouds themselves did not rain destruction upon those beneath. For every time one of the guns fired and missed from such a height, it crashed through forest and field and waves, damaging everything in its path.

"Freddie says Lady Hollys has a lightning pistol," Davey said a little breathlessly. "Imagine a gun like that. No ball to kill everything on its way down."

William would lay a wager that the crew of Number Seven would wish they had such a thing, had they known of it. In the next moment, the big Daimlers roared and the captain wheeled her about, but too late. The middle ship of the trio fired, and caught her in the stern. It was a tactic that had worked all too well with their own vessel, piercing the fuselage and rearmost of the three internal gasbags. Even at half a mile distant, they could hear the scream of the escaping lifting gas.

A puff of steam from the stern, and Number Seven pushed its way toward the horrified spectators in the tree. Heading southwest with a definite list. Running for its home field before any more damage was done.

Number Nineteen covered its retreat, the Gatling gun in the stern tracing a trail of holes across the bow of the fuselage of the third pirate vessel, while Nineteen's heavy forward guns fired on the stern of the one pursuing Number Seven.

"A direct hit!" Davey cheered, remembering just in time to keep his grip on his branch.

The ball pierced the pirate fuselage on a nearly horizontal trajectory from stern to bow, ripping through one gasbag after another.

"It got all three," Oscar said in wonder. "She'll go down for certain."

Number Seven raced over their heads and William could swear that one of the men pressed to the viewing port saw them, for he whirled about, gesturing frantically. But there was no way now to come to their aid. No way to do anything but race for the city of Victoria and hope they would make it.

The doomed vessel holed by Number Nineteen fell screaming from the sky, almost close enough for William to reach out and touch its deflating fuselage. The gondola scraped the tops of the neighboring trees, snapping them off like match sticks, before it plummeted past the little beach where they had gathered oysters and plunged into the sound with a *whump!* like the liquid thunder of a breaching whale.

The gondola hit first, the combined weight of gasbags and fuselage flung over its bow dragging it out into the middle of the sound before spreading over it and preventing its crew from escaping. Its entire suffocating weight pressed the gondola under.

"Can the crew get out?" Davey croaked.

"It is a hundred feet at least to swim underwater, if they can even get the hatches open," Oscar said grimly.

"Where is the third ship?" William could not watch the ship drown. He scanned the sky through the topmost branches. "Where has it gone?"

The boom of the cannon sounded once more as the third ship stooped from its greater height upon Number Nineteen, as if enraged that it had fought back. The ball pierced Nineteen's fuselage, but for a wonder, it did not collapse. But with a second shot, the entire rear quarter of Nineteen's gondola was blown off, and the body of the engineer cartwheeled through the air to land with a bone-breaking splash in the sound, the starboard engine smashing into the water scant yards behind him.

"They must go down," William said in horror. "They cannot survive such damage."

"They must not, and they will," Oscar said between his teeth.

Number Nineteen fled, its one engine roaring for all it was worth, the ship doing its best to get out of range before it was holed for certain with the next shot. And by some miracle, a great gust of wind came out of the north carrying a blast of rain and pushed the middle ship off its pursuit course just enough for the next shot from its gun to fly wide.

Nineteen did not hesitate. Every ounce of power was applied to the remaining engine, and it fled into the lowering clouds, disappearing as surely as a candle winks out to leave a room in darkness.

Their day's work at staying dry was undone in less than ten seconds as the rain beat down on their unprotected heads. All William could see was the two remaining ships, slowing to circle the downed carcass of the ship in the water. No splashing of surfacing men showed in the whitecaps kicked up by the wind. No figures clung to the floating canvas, or even the driftwood driven into the sound by the swells.

"We must get down and find another hiding place while they are occupied," Oscar said. "Davey, are you up for it?"

"Aye," the boy said, his gaze fixed on the ships.

William said, "I thought you said we were safer in the trees."

"Not these trees. Not now that they know where we are."

The ship that had been in the middle—the one with the

gunner who had already toyed with Davey's life—had completed its circuit of the downed vessel and was coming about.

Davey released his branch and started down. "Better hurry," he said. "They're coming back to finish the job."

CHAPTER 5

VICTORIA

12:45 p.m.

When pressed, Inspector Kent allowed that the two rescue ships would likely not return until nearly sunset. "They will waste no time, I assure you," he told the Linden family, "to report and, we hope, to deliver the crew of Number Thirteen safely. There is no reason for you to sit here and fret. Perhaps you might enjoy a walk about the harbor. Look in the shops. Take tea at the Empress Hotel, perhaps. It is the finest hotel in the Columbia Territory."

"I cannot sit in a hotel drinking tea, not knowing whether my fiancé is dead or alive," Daisy said.

Freddie was surprised at her sister's bluntness, but couldn't help agreeing with her. What a suggestion!

The inspector gazed at Daisy with an expression Freddie could not read. Or perhaps it was no expression at all, other than scrupulous politeness. "It will help to pass the time," he said. "And take your mind off the situation."

"We are not such trivial females as can be distracted with

44

tea and shopping," Freddie said with some asperity. "We should prefer to remain here in case there is news."

"I am afraid I cannot permit such a distraction to my men," Inspector Kent said. "You see how they prefer to be here in the mess wasting time, rather than at their posts carrying out their duties."

"Perhaps they are worried for their fellow officers, too," Papa offered.

"They may be worried and attend their duty at the same time, sir."

"Whereas in the absence of duty, we have only worry to occupy us," Daisy said. "Very well. We will take a brief walk about the harbor, and return within the hour to take up our watch at the field."

A muscle flexed in his jaw, but Inspector Kent merely inclined his head in the slightest bow allowed by the human body, and departed the mess hall, his back straight and his steps so precise they became a march.

"Perhaps I was mistaken," Freddie said, watching him pass out of sight. "That cannot be Oscar's father. He shows no more emotion than if he were reading of these events in the newspaper."

"Perhaps he does not wish to show favoritism before the other aeronauts," Daisy suggested.

"That I could understand. But this is taking fairness all the way to utter indifference."

"I wonder if their relationship might be strained," Papa said. "In which case, it is none of our business."

"It is my business, if he is to be—" Freddie stopped, remembering suddenly that Oscar Kent had not yet kissed her, much less proposed marriage, and that in fact, the inspector was no closer to being her father-in-law than the Prince Consort.

Daisy, thankfully, said no more, not in front of a dozen aeronauts, all stealing glances in their direction while wolfing down their own stew and cheese toast. "Come," her sister said. "Let us restore order to the barracks by leaving it. At least for an hour."

In summer, the front of the government building would have been a mass of roses, laid out in orderly beds in lawns that were trimmed as carefully as any aeronaut's hair. The wide drive up to the front steps was bisected by a circle. Set in the middle were a pair of sculptures, boldly and beautifully worked. Freddie tilted her head. The figures were perched one upon another—a bear, surely, and a whale, and a salmon. A fearsome eagle glared near the top of one, and upon the other a figure only slightly less fearsome—an osprey. At the very top was a round, placid shape with huge stylized eyes— the moon. And there on the other, that must be the sun.

"Breathtaking," Daisy said softly, her artist's eye delighting in the details of claw and fin and likely wishing she could take out her sketchbook on the spot. "I should love to know the story they tell. I wonder if Lady Dunsmuir knows."

"I expect so," Freddie said. "She was, after all, born along these shores. And even now she occupies a position of authority in the federation of original nations."

"They must have been carved in place. I cannot imagine the difficulty of transporting something so large and heavy," Papa said as they passed the regal pair. "It would task an airship's engines—even *Swan*'s engines, I think."

"Have you flown on *Swan*, Papa?" Daisy asked, taking his arm as they made their way along the road that fronted the harbor, bristling with cargo docks and fishing boats, and hosting several yachts and steamships.

"I have, my dear. The two Captains Hollys flew me from the water meadows of Las Vegas to Reno, where I took up my search for you and your dear mother." He sighed. "As it turned out, my mind was so muddled then it is a wonder I was not killed at that crossroads of two disparate civilizations. All I knew was that Santa Fe had been our destination before the attack, so some force within me prompted me to return to that point."

"That is where we, too, began our search for you," Freddie put in, taking his other arm. "But imagine your traveling aboard *Swan*. We booked passage on her when we arrived in New York. It was our good fortune that Captain Hollys was bound for Denver."

"I say, are you speaking of Alice or Ian Hollys?" said a male voice behind them. An unmistakeable voice, half Cockney and half Scots.

Freddie turned in surprise. The voice was so familiar, but—

The young man was about the same age as she was, with green eyes and hair that looked as though he had recently been in a strong wind. He wore a short belted khaki jacket such as aeronauts wore, with his goggles pushed up on his cap and the navigator's compass on the points of his collar.

"I'm sorry," Daisy said uncertainly, clearly half-recognizing him as well. "Could you remind me ...?"

He took in Papa at a glance, and those eyes widened. "Dutch! It cannot be."

Papa's mouth fell open. "Jake Fletcher?"

"It is indeed. Miss Linden, you've done it. You've found your father!"

Jake Fletcher. Navigator aboard *Swan*. One of Maggie Polgarth's friends in London, if Freddie remembered correctly. Goodness, she'd last seen him months ago aboard ship, and here he was pumping Papa's hand as though they were old friends. And Papa had remembered his name! This was progress indeed.

"We have, Mr. Fletcher," Freddie said, feeling the first glimmer of warmth since they had left the RCAP mess hall.

Daisy offered her hand. "What an unexpected pleasure to see you here. Our father has recovered his real name now—Professor Rudolph Linden."

"I am so very glad to see you after all these miles," Papa told him, looking pleased.

"And I you, Professor." Jake grinned, a raffish smile, but all the same, there was a glint in his eye that told Freddie a person would not want to be on the wrong side of him. "I must say, you're looking much better than when you were first released from a Californio gaol."

"I'm afraid it is not so long since I have been released from a Columbia Territory gaol. I seem to have bad luck in that department," Papa said wryly. "But in Port Townsend they did not hesitate to feed me, which I cannot say for the other place. Jake, if you are the navigator aboard *Swan*, why are you here? We saw her lift only this morning."

"I was due for land leave. The captains are paying a visit to the Northern Light to visit Mrs Nellie Benton Embry and her husband, and to present themselves as escort to the royal couple on their way here. Neither of those shindigs seemed my business, or worth my going all the way to Edmonton for, and those two can sail *Swan* easily."

"The Duke and Duchess's loss is our gain, then," Daisy said, sounding immensely cheered by this chance meeting of someone they knew in a strange city.

"How long have you been here, then, if you saw *Swan* lift?" Jake asked.

Freddie glanced at her father. "Four hours?" He nodded.

"Only four! I've been here two days and feel as though it has been a year. It is just enough like London or Edinburgh to make me homesick, with none of the people I love here to make me happy." A bleak expression passed through his eyes.

"Have you heard from Maggie?" Freddie asked, as seagulls dipped and mewed over a fishing boat coming in to its berth. "We were friends, you may remember, at school."

"That's right." Jake's face warmed to something close to handsomeness at the mention of Maggie's name. "I hope you will be happy to know that she is now my intended."

"Is she indeed!" Freddie said. She had always suspected that Maggie's heart belonged to someone, but the latter had never confided in her to that deep an extent. "I am very happy to hear it."

"We cannot become engaged until she graduates, but we are content to wait. She has begun her third year of study, so not long now. Genetics is her field. But to answer your question, yes, I had a letter when we were in Charlottetown last month."

"Goodness. Genetics. Something far beyond my poor brain," Freddie said.

"You do yourself an injustice," Papa remonstrated. "Who but my two girls solved the judge's murder?"

"Murder?" Jake's brows rose.

"It is a tale for a hot fire and a long dinner," Daisy said hastily. "We will not keep you from your land leave, Mr. Fletcher. I'm afraid we are here under rather gloomy circumstances and our time is no longer our own."

"I am no stranger to gloomy circumstances," he said, looking among them as though their faces alone might tell him what was the matter. "Are you well? May I do something for you?"

"Oh, yes, we are all well," Daisy assured him. "That is, half our party is well. The other half, I am afraid—"

"—has been captured by Pig Iron Kelly's air pirates, and the RCAP are at this moment undertaking a rescue." Freddie did not hesitate to lay out the circumstances with such crispness the words positively made slashes in the air. It was rather satisfying.

Jake's only reaction was a blink. "When did this happen?"

"Only a few hours ago," Papa said. "We lifted from Port Townsend just before nine this morning, in my future son-in-law's conveyance—"

Another blink. Jake's gaze searched those of Daisy and Freddie, clearly wondering to which of them the future son-in-law belonged.

"My fiancé, William Barnicott, and our ward, Davey, were aboard the RCAP airship piloted by Corporal Oscar Kent," Daisy explained in answer to the silent question. "Yes, our family has seen many changes since we flew with you."

"The pilot—that isn't Inspector Kent's son?"

"You know them?" Freddie blurted in surprise.

"I cannot say I know them, exactly," Jake admitted, "but there was a ball given at Cary Castle for Alice and Ian night before last, and the inspector was there, holding up his bit of the wall with a great deal more presence than I ever could. We had a brief conversation when he saw my uniform."

"Ah. Well, he dispatched two ships to go to our friends' rescue," Papa said, "and so instead of walking circles on the field at the barracks, we were ordered to go to a hotel and take tea." His voice carried all the disgust that Freddie herself felt.

Jake tilted his head. "Not exactly the rescue maneuver I would have employed."

"We were not permitted a maneuver of any kind," Daisy said bitterly. "We were shuffled out of the way like so many children—though I must say I know one child at least who is quite capable of pulling off a rescue. And has done."

"I know a fair number of such children myself," Jake said. "So, what is your plan?"

"Do as we're told, I suppose," Freddie told him. "Until the ships return with news—or our friends."

"And if they return empty-handed?"

Jake had just put words to the fear that was even now tumbling Freddie's nourishing lunch about in her stomach like a whirlpool. "I don't know," she whispered. "But—but Osc —the inspector's own son—surely they will pull out all the stops to see him safe."

"I'm sure they will," Jake said in a tone Freddie thought was meant to be comforting, but only made her feel worse. "But I've heard things about Pig Iron Kelly. He reminds me very much of a man I knew in the Texican Territories years ago."

"An air pirate?" Freddie asked. Had *Swan*, too, had a run-in with such a criminal?

"As it happens, yes. He threw me out of an airship. In flight."

Daisy gasped. Freddie clapped a hand to her mouth.

"Luckily I landed in a lake. You cannot put anything past these men who have no regard for anything but the bottomless pit of their own greed and selfishness." He paused, having clearly just observed that his ruminations were only increasing their distress. "I'm sorry. That was thoughtless of me."

Daisy shook her head. "It's all right. It can't be worse than our own dreadful imaginings."

"Tell me, where are you staying?" he asked with a change of tone.

That was a poser. Freddie, for one, had not given it a moment's consideration. She could not think beyond the return of the rescue party. When no one replied, she offered, "Aboard the conveyance, I suppose, at the civic airfield."

"The what now?" Jake looked amused. "Is that what you call your ship?"

"She isn't a ship," Papa said. "She is William's creation—"

"And Tobin's, Papa," Daisy reminded him. "Our engineer friend in the Navapai village above Santa Fe."

"The pair of them have taken a vehicle that was part apothecary shop and part steam landau, and turned it into a sort of gondola, with a balloon, propellers and vanes powered by a Crockett engine," their father went on. "So it is not a proper airship."

Jake laughed. "In Alice's mind, nothing running a Crockett engine is a proper airship."

"I mean to say, it is a ... conveyance. It will never outsail a ship, but it did a very commendable five knots coming here over open water."

"And it has saved our lives a time or two," Daisy said in its defense.

"The RCAP vessel was escorting us," Freddie added. "The pirates attacked it as though they had been waiting for it, and ignored us altogether. For which I suppose I should be grateful. Though I feel anything but."

"I should say so," Jake said. "Well, you're welcome to come home with me. Since Alice has taken my cabin with her, they're putting me up in a boarding house just up there." He nodded up the broad thoroughfare just to the left of the Birdcages. "I have the whole second floor, and two meals a day to boot."

"They took an entire floor just for you?" Freddie asked. "That is very generous."

"I think they felt sorry for me, choosing to be left out of all the festivities," Jake said with another laugh. "Perhaps they thought I would bring home a crowd of mates and throw a party."

"Would a pair of weepy women and an academic do?" Daisy said. Freddie had not heard her sister sound so pathetic since the very beginning of their journey. "Because if so, we should be very happy to accept your hospitality. And Freddie, what a fortunate thing that I happen to have my zinnia pin right here in my reticule."

Freddie had hers in her own, because one never knew when one might need the help of an absent friend. They pinned the little enamel flowers to their lapels and followed their guide up the slope from the harbor.

Under the branches of the two maple trees in the front

garden, Jake's boarding house boasted a clear view out the parlor window of the entire expanse of the RCAP landing field. To their immense satisfaction, the boarding-house keeper was indeed a member of the society of absent friends, and with one glance at their zinnia pins, took Freddie and Daisy to her bosom both literally and figuratively. Nothing was too good for them, no accommodation too trivial.

"I am Mrs Birch," she said, her eyes aglow with delight. "Eleanor Birch, a widow these four years, and I have only yesterday had a letter from Selena Chang in Bodie. What fun it will be to share the news with everyone that the Linden family is staying in my house! For of course I have heard all about you," she confided, her dimples denting unlined cheeks. "Now that you have found your father, you clever girls, all that remains is for you to solve another murder while you are with me."

"*Another* murder—?" Jake managed.

"Indeed, Mr. Fletcher. What famous company you have found yourself in! Not as famous as Sir Ian and Lady Hollys, mind you, or Lord and Lady Dunsmuir, but for we humble women of the western territories, the exchange of our letters lately is quite like having our own *Tales of a Medicine Man.*" She paused. "Or ought I to say *Tales of Mysterious Ladies?*"

It felt good to laugh.

Daisy said, "My dear Mrs Birch, never mind us—I may tell you for your ears only that my fiancé is the author—the Educated Gentleman himself. That is why we are here—he and our friends were shot down by Pig Iron Kelly over the archipelago. I cannot tell you how happy I am that the airfield is in full view of your house—we are at this moment on tenterhooks, waiting for the sight of the RCAP rescue vessels' return."

Now it was Mrs Birch's turn to cover her beautifully shaped mouth with the hand on which a plain gold band still reposed. "No," she breathed. "Your fiancé is An Educated Gentleman? Truly?"

"He informs me so, quite reliably," Daisy said. The fact that he had been shot down by pirates seemed to be quite of a piece in this lady's eyes—and altogether expected of the Medicine Man.

"Goodness. Think of the tale he will have to tell!" She clutched Daisy's arm. "When he is safely returned, you must permit me to host a small soirée for the two of you. Why, it will be the most thrilling thing since the Lieutenant-Governor arrived!"

"If—I mean, when that welcome event occurs, we will be your guests most happily," Daisy promised, shooting a quick glance at Freddie that the latter interpreted as hope that she was not tempting fate.

Freddie hoped so, too.

CHAPTER 6

There was no sign yet of the rescue ships by the time Papa and Jake returned with the conveyance, which Mrs Birch insisted be moored in her enormous back garden. Neatly mulched vegetable beds and herbaceous borders gave way to a spreading lawn and an apple orchard, the whole property extending to the next street over.

"In the summer, you know, we often dine *al fresco* out here," she said, waving a hand to encompass the garden, "but as you are my only guests at present, there is no reason why you must hire a landau to take you to the public airfield should you need to travel."

"Mrs Birch, this is so generous," Daisy said. "You must allow us to compensate you for the rooms, and the moorage."

"Nonsense," Jake said, looping the last rope around a mooring iron. "The rooms are paid for. Why should they be empty when you need them?"

"My thoughts exactly," Mrs Birch said. "And the lawn, too. Now, bring in your luggage, and then we will have tea in the parlor and keep an eye on the RCAP field together while you tell me all about your adventures."

A shadow passed overhead as Daisy took her valise from Papa at the rear of the conveyance, and her stomach plunged.

Only a cloud.

The weather was changing, the clouds massing. They would have rain again soon. *Oh, William, I hope you are somewhere snug and dry and safe.*

She was so jumpy that at this rate she would be painting dear Mrs Birch's teacups, not drinking from them. The tea was hot and delicious, the cake plate piled high with tarts and slices. Daisy shared her sketchbook with Mrs Birch, and as the lady exclaimed over the landscapes Daisy had painted in San Francisco, she and Freddie told the tale of the earthquake and the subsequent disaster to the city—to say nothing of the attempted political coup—that had followed Papa's departure on the *Barbara Carol.*

"I am very glad you took passage on that steamship, Papa," Daisy told her father, giving his hand a squeeze. "You left in the nick of time, though of course we had no way of knowing that until much later, with the assistance of our friends in the Canton district."

"I cannot agree," he said sadly. "Had I waited for the next northbound steamer, I might not have been on the beach that morning and seen—"

"But that is a tale for another day," Freddie said hastily. "We shall be like Scheherazade, telling our stories to earn our tea."

"I hope this will be the only day you are obliged to do so," Mrs Birch replied, her sympathetic gaze upon Papa. "Surely your friends will be returned to you by sunset."

"You are kind, madame," he said. "I very much hope so."

"I cannot leave this room," Daisy said fretfully. Her very breath seemed to come short, as though she were perpetually holding it. "Will you forgive me if I paint your teacups while I keep watch?"

"You may paint the entire room if you like," Mrs Birch said. "I did notice a preponderance of teacups in this sketch-book." She handed it over with a smile.

"Painting them soothes her," Daisy heard Freddie say as she fetched two tumblers of water. She arranged her paintbox and brushes on yesterday's newspaper spread on a side table, all with a good view of the window, and began. The pattern of birds on the cups was both calming and complex, and as conversation flowed around her, she found herself falling into the pleasure of the task.

When the teacups were completed and the real ones cleared away, and Papa had built up the fire, Daisy turned to a fresh page and began a portrait of Jake. He was in profile, his watchful gaze on the sky and the airfield, the cool, cloudy light perfect. She worked quickly, for it would not be long before an active man such as he would be up and about his business. She mixed up a satisfying light brown for the shadows and lights in his hair, and used them for the shadows under his khaki collar, too.

And when it was complete and mostly dry, she tucked a bit of onionskin between the pages to prevent smears, and turned to her landlady. Here was a subject who was neither watchful nor still. Her business was the comfort of her guests, and it was only when she fell into conversation with Papa that Daisy could capture the finer details of mouth and eyes. There were crows' feet at the corners that spoke of laughter … or perhaps a tendency to watch the skies for an airship's return. Mrs Birch could not be much more than forty—possibly not even that. Her reddish-gold hair was piled on top of her head in waves that were a pleasure to paint, with none of the annoying false fronts of curls that had inexplicably come back into fashion. Her eyes were a hazel the color of tea, and a flush of color rode her cheekbones as she thrilled to the story Papa was telling about Bodie.

Daisy lifted her gaze to find Freddie's own eyes upon her. Her sister tilted her head toward the conversing pair. One eyebrow went up in a silent question.

She rinsed her brush thoughtfully. It had been a long, long time since she had seen Papa talking with such pleasure to any woman but Mama. But it was impossible—he had just found out his wife had died a few short months ago. When did the year of mourning begin? At the time of the actual death? Or upon the bereaved person's first knowledge of it?

Freddie was waiting. Daisy shook her head.

"Daisy." Jake's voice was as still as a pond before the stone hits the surface. And then it struck. "I see two airships on a short approach."

3:10 p.m.

Daisy managed not to drop the sketchbook in her hurry to reach the window, laying it open at the half-finished portrait so it would not smear and thrusting her brush into the glass of water. Then all she could see were the two ships limping through the skies on a short approach from the southeast.

She made a sound and clutched Jake's sleeve. "What has happened to them?"

Now the others were crowded at the window, Mrs Birch drawing a horrified breath.

"They have been holed," Papa said hoarsely. "There, to the stern on the one. The third gasbag has completely collapsed. And look—half the gondola is missing on the other! How did they get across the straits in weather like this without going down altogether?"

"They must have skilled captains," Jake said. "Come. Let us go at once."

Daisy and Freddie snatched the jackets of their walking costumes off the hall tree and were halfway out the door before Mrs Birch could snatch up their hats and shove them into their hands. Daisy pinned hers on as she half walked, half ran across the thoroughfare, and when she reached the field she abandoned walking altogether, Freddie hot on her heels. Jake and Papa followed, leaving Mrs Birch on her front verandah with her hands clasped to her chest, vainly calling after them that they ought to have an umbrella.

By the time they reached the rear of the barracks, Inspector Kent was marching down the steps. He stood at parade rest, feet planted apart in the grass, hands behind his back, as they ran up, panting and disheveled.

"I expected you earlier," he said, watching the ships attempt to set down when their maneuverability was so compromised. The ground crew scattered to catch the ropes and winch them down manually.

"We have found accommodation," Papa said when neither Daisy nor Freddie could reply to such a banality. "At Mrs Birch's boarding house, there." He pointed across the field, where the lady was watching anxiously from the verandah.

"Accommodation," the inspector repeated. "I see. You have chosen well—Mrs Birch's establishment is well regarded."

There was no reply to make to this, and Jake did not seem inclined to be brought to the inspector's recollection. He could reintroduce himself if he liked—Daisy's entire being was focused on the ships.

The two were secured, the shout given. The gangway of the first came down and the aeronauts immediately marched to the other bearing two stretchers. Out of the blasted, yawning hole in the damaged gondola, which once contained the gangway, two groaning men were let down to the grass. They were swiftly loaded on to the stretchers and borne away, presumably to sick bay. Two men who were still mobile enough to go on their own feet followed, supported by their brethren.

The two captains and the remaining crew members formed lines as before between the two ships, but oh, what a difference. What a gaping, terrible absence lay between the lines.

She must not retch. Or faint. Or weep. She must be calm.

"Report," Inspector Kent said.

The captain of the least damaged ship saluted. "We located the wreckage of Number Thirteen on the north end of Whitby Island, as expected, sir. After reconnaissance, we determined the gondola was undamaged, and it was likely the crew survived."

Daisy sucked in a lungful of air and the black spots encroaching on her vision retreated.

"In addition, it appeared that part of the fuselage had been cut and carried off, presumably as temporary shelter."

Oh, what a good idea. Daisy could almost breathe normally.

"As we came about, preparing to make a visual pass over that end of the island, we were attacked by three of Pig Iron Kelly's ships in an arrow formation, using a steep dive out of the cloud cover. They carried mounted guns, and Number Seven's fuselage was holed almost before we could engage."

"Where was the watch?" Inspector Kent demanded, his face impassive.

"On duty, sir, and giving the alarm, but we could not power up the engines quickly enough. They fell right out of the clouds, sir."

"Continue."

The captain of the ship with half a gondola left saluted. "We engaged with the enemy and drew their fire long enough for Seven to retreat and head for Victoria. In the process, we were holed and lost our engineer over the water. But before that, we were able to gut one of the enemy ships from bow to stern. She went down in the sound with, we believe, all hands lost."

"That's something," the inspector remarked, almost to himself. Then, louder, "Any sign of Corporal Kent and the passengers of Number Thirteen?"

"Yes, sir," one of the aeronauts said, saluting. "I caught a glimpse of a boy and two men in a treetop, two or three miles west of the crash site. They witnessed the dogfight, but by then we were not only badly damaged but being pursued. We were unable to stop and pick them up. And lucky not to wind up in the salt chuck, sir."

"Clearly," Inspector Kent said. "It is also quite clear that our last two ships are out of commission for the foreseeable future. Thank you, gentlemen, for making the attempt."

The crew and two captains saluted and marched double time for the barracks, leaving their commander to contemplate the destruction of his airships … and his rescue plan.

"A boy and two men in a treetop!" Daisy said to Freddie in an undertone. "Is this not good news?"

"It is," Freddie said, her own breath coming fast. "It means they are unharmed."

"How long can they remain unharmed, is the question," Papa said. "Mr Fletcher, have you any experience of these islands?"

"None, sir," Jake said. "We had a wee run-in with Pig Iron Kelly just north of Port Townsend last year, but he will not thank me for the memory. Captain Alice took out one of his engines with a bolt from her lightning pistol, leaving the ship adrift and no hope but to fall out of the sky. She gives no quarter, does our captain, having more experience than the average person with air pirates."

"How I wish we had such a pistol," Daisy groaned. "And I do not even know what it is."

Inspector Kent remained silent. Daisy might have thought he was lost in making plans to secure his son, had not his gaze lay upon them with something close to impatience. Did he wish them to leave so that he might go in and brief his remaining men on their next steps?

"I am very sorry for your losses," she ventured, when his gaze moved to her. "I do not wish to—"

"I do not see why *you* should be sorry," he said. "I lay the loss of three of Her Majesty's ships and at least one skilled aeronaut at my son's door."

Freddie drew a sharp breath, so softly only Daisy heard it. The gasp of a woman taking a mortal blow.

How dared he! Daisy's temper flared.

"From where I stand, Corporal Kent is very capably keeping my fiancé and our ward out of harm's way," she said crisply. "And how he could be blamed for your captains' being surprised by a wily and experienced pirate when he is up in a tree is more than I can understand."

"I cannot expect a young lady of your tender years to do any such thing."

Oh, this was tossing coals in the firebox now.

"I assure you, my years are tender no longer. I'll wager I've faced down death more times in the past four months than you have in your entire career," she snapped. "What I want to know is, what is the next plan to recover your son and my future family?"

"Daisy," Papa whispered, completely taken aback by her loss of manners.

"I will meet with my men, but an alternate plan will take time," the inspector said.

"How much time? Until tomorrow morning?" Daisy would not allow him to fob her off with vague estimations.

"No. I expect it will take three or four days to locate a steamship, to say nothing of a captain willing to put in at Whitby to bargain with Pig Iron Kelly on your behalf."

A steamship! *Bargain?*

He must have seen the incredulity in her face, for he went on, "I have no more airships to spare. Our situation, in fact, is particularly grave should Kelly take it into his head to attack Victoria now."

"Is there some danger of that?" Jake asked. "Has he made threats?"

"He keeps patrols in the air constantly," the inspector said. "Most of the time they are too far away to engage, but even a coward may count ships in an airfield. And choose his moment."

"But—a *steamship*—" Daisy could not imagine anything more unwieldy or slow when speed and surprise were urgently called for.

"If you have a better suggestion, Miss Linden, you have my complete attention."

His sarcasm scraped her lacerated emotions like sandpaper.

"I *suggest* that you spend some time meditating on your son's good qualities, and his worthiness of your regard and care," she replied, her tone so polite it scratched. "Because if he does not come back from this voyage, you will spend the rest of your life regretting every word you have said about him. And, I have no doubt, *to* him." She turned her back upon his rigid form. "Come, Freddie. We have seen all that we came for, and quite a lot I wish I hadn't."

Without a word, Freddie took her arm and they marched away across the field. Papa sketched a bow and followed them. Jake did not even bother himself to that extent; despite their acquaintance, Inspector Kent had not acknowledged him in the first place.

Mrs Birch took them in as they mounted the steps to the verandah of her boarding house. "What news?" she managed. "Marcus was in a temper, even I could see that."

Marcus? Their landlady was on a first-name basis with the RCAP inspector?

Daisy would not glance at Papa to see how he had taken what was all but a declaration. Marcus, *hmph*. One may as well entertain romantic notions of a piece of granite.

"He was indeed in a temper," Freddie said. "He blames his son for this disaster. Every bit of it. And now I do not believe we can count upon the RCAP at all. For the best solution he had was to hire a steamship and a captain willing to bargain with Pig Iron Kelly for their lives!"

"Oh dear," Mrs Birch said faintly. "That does not sound very … workable."

"It sounds as though he expects them to be captured," Jake said, his tone tinged with disgust. "And that he has a very low opinion of his son."

Freddie turned and went into the house without another word.

CHAPTER 7

3:50 p.m.

"Please excuse me," Daisy murmured, and followed her sister inside.

She found Freddie in the sitting room with the glasses of water Daisy had been using in her hands. "Are you going to paint any more?"

"No, dearest. Thank you."

Silently, Freddie took the soiled glasses out to the kitchen, and Daisy followed with the tea things. The others came in and left them alone—even Mrs Birch, whose sanctuary they were invading. They had washed and dried the dishes and returned to the parlor to collect Daisy's sketchbook and paintbox before Freddie spoke again.

"I never thought to meet a man with so little feeling for his only family." She seated herself in the chair beside the fire, not the one she had occupied before, next to the window.

"Oh, Oscar is not his only family," Mrs Birch said. "You must make some allowances, my dear."

"I think not," Daisy said. "He is absolutely horrible on the subject of his son. I believe that if we were not here importuning him at every moment, he would shrug and leave Corporal Kent to the pirates's mercies altogether."

"Now you do him an injustice," Mrs Birch said reproachfully. "He is not as bad as all that. Marcus has had his share of burdens to bear. I am afraid this last one has simply crushed his spirit. You saw before you a shell of a man, with nothing left to hold himself up but his self-discipline and his need to appear calm before his men."

Silence met this declaration.

Then Papa said, "It appears you know him much better than we do, Madame."

Poor Papa. He was yielding the field before he had even set foot upon it.

"I should think so," Mrs Birch said. "We are family. His wife, Clementine, and my husband, Montrose, were brother and sister. God rest their souls."

Papa, standing at the window with his hands clasped behind his back, turned in surprise. "Family?"

"Yes indeed. Do sit down, Professor. I am in quite as much a state about my nephew as you are about your family-to-be, I assure you, but watching that field will do you no good."

Papa sank into the corner of the sofa next to Daisy, completely bereft of words.

Daisy began to regret losing her self-control in front of the inspector.

"But how can he say such things?" Freddie burst out. "He blames Oscar for the loss of three ships and the death of that poor man. Those are the pirates' fault, not his!"

Mrs Birch clasped her knee under the fine olive-green

gabardine of her skirt and nodded sadly. "Of course they are. But when a man is confronted a second time with the most painful event of his life, he may be excused if his tongue runs away with him."

Freddie stared at her, waiting.

"It was Oscar, you see, who was at the helm of a training ship when he took his mother up. He was only a cadet. She was a brilliant, laughing thing, always ready for adventure—and so capable! Why, when Marcus was posted to Edmonton, Clementine was out teaching little Oscar and his two sisters how to snowshoe and they were surprised by a wolf. What should she do but raise the rifle to her shoulder and shoot it through the eye before it could attack her children? Oh, there was no moss on Clemmie. She was the perfect wife for an RCAP officer. Marcus worshipped the ground she walked on."

"But … the training ship?" Freddie persisted, evidently not to be distracted by the news that Corporal Kent had sisters. "What happened?"

Mrs Birch sighed. "This was in Charlottetown, just before the dear boy graduated from the flight academy. Oscar was to do his practicum—a solo flight—and did not know there had been trouble with the engine. The ground crew should never have left the ship on the landing field, and were disciplined for it, but …" Another sigh. "He was permitted one passenger. It was supposed to be the training officer, but everyone knew Clemmie could fly a ship as well as any of them. He took her up—the engine failed—and they landed so far out in the channel between the island and the mainland that the rescue ship could not reach them in time."

"And only Oscar survived." Jake was being drawn into the tale now.

"He had the benefit of rigorous training and was in excellent physical condition. He did all he could to keep his mother out of the waves, but after they were rescued, she took pneumonia. The same terrible condition claimed my Montrose, as it happens, only under vastly different circumstances."

Daisy and Freddie exchanged a glance, imagining the terrible scene—the frantic son, the relentless sea.

"And his father cannot forgive him." Mrs Birch dashed a tear from her cheek. "It was ten years ago at least, and he cannot even bring himself to look poor Oscar in the eyes. When the boy was posted here, the first thing Marcus did was request a transfer out. But it was denied. So Oscar was dispatched to Port Townsend, and there he has been for four years, with no contact with his father outside of orders."

"How dreadfully sad," Freddie said. "For both of them."

"I cannot condone the things he said," Daisy said, "but since it is none of my nevermind, I suppose I will have to apologize for the things *I* said just now."

"Yes, I expect you will," Papa agreed.

Daisy frowned at him. She was not quite ready to be agreed with.

"Let us return to the main point," Papa went on. "Enjoyable as our hostess's company is—" He bowed to Mrs Birch from his seat. "—the situation is urgent. Something must be done. Are we to wait for a steamship to be engaged? Or ought we to take matters into our own hands?"

"Oh my, you cannot do that," Mrs Birch said, leaning forward in distress. "Will you put the steamship captain in the position of negotiating for six people instead of three?"

"Seven," Jake said. "Whatever you do, include me. I rather specialize in urgent situations."

"I do not know whether to be dismayed or relieved, Mr Fletcher," Daisy said. "But I am grateful. And I agree with Papa. The time has come to do something ourselves."

"What will you do?" Mrs Birch's lovely eyes were wide.

"We still have the conveyance," Papa said. "We know where Number Thirteen went down. All we have to do is float in unobserved, and mount our own search for our friends."

"Unobserved," Freddie repeated. "That will be the tricky part. Buff and scarlet stripes are rather noticeable."

"But we are small," Daisy said thoughtfully. "If our altitude is low and we use other islands for protection, we may just succeed. Especially if we fly at night."

"We'll need to make some preparations," Jake said. "My lightning pistol is useful, but not against a dozen men."

"You have a lightning pistol?" Daisy asked. "Why did you not say so before?"

"Because one doesn't admit to such things in front of RCAP officers," Jake said. "It's all very well for Captain Alice to have one. But I find that the fewer who know about mine, the less trouble I'm likely to see."

"I feel better already," Daisy said. "Come. Let us make a list. I should like to lift at sunset."

Whitby Island
5:05 p.m.

"We must keep moving." William got up and wiped his face. "If what Oscar says is true, we will face the greatest danger at the head of the sound, where the village is."

"Even a small band of men bivouacked there can prevent

us from reaching the southwest side of the island," Oscar said. "Come on, Davey." He offered his hand.

"I'm hungry," Davey moaned from under his canvas square. But he took the hand and allowed himself to be hauled to his feet.

It was nearly dark, and the tide was in. "It's a pity we cannot forage for more food," William observed. "But I wonder if any supplies might have washed ashore from the pirate wreck?"

Oscar's body stiffened. "I had not thought of that. Come. Let us venture out from under the eaves of the forest and have a look."

"The gondola wasn't holed like the RCAP ship," Davey objected. "If it's secure, how will food get out of the galley?"

"Perhaps the gondola wasn't secure," William said. "Do pirates obey the safety regulations required of commercial ships?"

Davey's face brightened in the gloom. "Let's hope not. Does cheese float?"

"Be careful," Oscar said, draping his canvas over himself more securely. "If there are survivors, they may have had the same thought, and the same question about cheese."

The incoming tide had dashed their hopes of oysters, but it had brought in the mass of the deflated fuselage, which was slowly and ponderously being washed against the rocks. Dragging along the bottom a hundred feet behind it was the gondola. A desolate clanging sound came from under the deep water as it repeatedly struck the rocks submerged far below.

"Pity it isn't daylight," Davey said. "The water is so clear here you can see twenty feet down."

William did not point out that if there were bodies caught in the rigging, the boy might not like what he saw. Their situation was dire enough without those horrors in his young imagination. "Let us make our way down the rocks," he suggested. "It is too difficult to see from here."

They scrambled down once again, though in their new position there was no beach to greet them. Only split and tumbled rocks waiting to seize a boot or twist an ankle. In the last of the fading light, even an optimist such as Davey could see that there were no boxes and crates of food bobbing in the water. No bottles that might contain something to warm their bellies. Nothing at all but the relentless wash of the waves and the desolate heaving and tearing of the fuselage.

"It was worth the attempt," Oscar admitted at last. "Come. Best to get out of sight."

It was more difficult making their way back up the tumbled fissures of the cliff in the wet twilight. William might have wondered if he had ever been so miserable had his mind not been so wholly consumed with not falling and breaking his neck. Davey scrambled up before him, and when Oscar reached the bank, he pulled the boy on to the wet grass before William followed. The three of them pulled out their canvas and sat huddled there, panting and making certain all limbs and digits were accounted for.

"Well now, what have we here?" A voice boomed out of the dark and nearly stopped William's heart.

"Wreckers, Sarge, I'll be bound," came a second voice.

William's eyes were dazzled by the strongest moonglobes he had ever seen shining mercilessly into their faces.

"Wreckers." William could see no faces behind the bright lights, but he could hear the disgust. "What have you got that doesn't belong to you, eh?" The voice was a resonant basso. Whoever this Sarge was, he was still probably an abuser of women. And a wrecker of ships.

William got his mouth working even as his stomach clenched. "Nothing. There were no signs of life down—"

"Shut up!" Someone else's boot found his shoulder and knocked him over. "Get up."

"You're the crew of that thrice-damned RCAP ship up on the point?" Sarge demanded.

He might demand, but William decided that since he'd been told to shut up, that's exactly what he would do. The question had to be rhetorical in any case. Oscar was still wearing his uniform, torn and soaked though it was.

"Pathetic. Search them and bring them along."

In the confusion, William felt someone fumble with his hand, then press something small into it.

His fingers closed on a ring. Oscar's mother's diamond ring.

But what in heaven's name was he to do with it? He had mere seconds to conceal it somewhere. Under a rock? Ram it into the dirt, where they might never locate it again?

Davey clung to him, his eyes huge and glittering in the fractious, swinging light. The sleeve of his jacket was torn, too, poor boy. What an unthreatening trio they made, as ragged as any beggars and it had only been a day since—

Wait. The *lined* sleeve.

William gripped Davey's shoulder and with his finger and thumb, slid the ring into the two-inch hole where the fabric had pulled out, like Oscar's jacket. Then he kept his hand there, as though he had meant to do so all along.

Davey looked up, and his fingers closed around the wrist

of his sleeve, where he had clearly just felt the ring come to rest under the lining.

And then someone tore their canvas squares out of their hands and threw them to the ground. "Won't need these where you're going. March!"

If any of the readers of the *Tales of a Medicine Man* ever thirsted for an account of a forced march through the darkness, they were going to be doomed to disappointment. William vowed to himself that if he survived, he would never resurrect this night in prose. Living through it once was going to be bad enough.

He had no idea how long they marched, only that Davey's legs gave out and he fell over a mossy log, draped there in exhaustion like a corpse over a horse's back. A pirate raised his fist and without thinking, William caught it.

"Don't," was all he had the breath for. The pirate must have seen the resolve in his face, for he yanked his hand free. William picked Davey up and slung him over his shoulder. The pirate could have struck both of them, but he only shrugged and joined his companions. And the endless nightmare began again.

He and Davey had the fair end of the bargain. The pirates took delight in pushing Oscar to his knees, in tripping him, in using the trail in any way they could to make him miserable, as though if he were injured, they could in good conscience put him down like a lamed animal.

But Oscar would not give them that satisfaction. When the search party finally marched through the outskirts of a village, he was still on his feet. Somehow.

The rain began again with such vehemence that William

was certain it would wash all the mud off them. He stumbled, then caught himself before Davey could fall.

"I'm … all right," he thought he heard the boy mumble.

Sarge waved a meaty hand at an edifice built into the hillside that had a door but no windows. "In there. Then it's supper for us, boys."

They were tossed inside unceremoniously and the door slammed and locked behind them.

The ruckus of shouts and laughter faded away. So, a village. Had they captured it? Or built it themselves? Was this the one at the head of the sound Oscar had spoken of? For some reason, William had assumed pirates lived on their ships, not among the ground-bound.

It didn't matter. What mattered was their own lives.

The interior of the gaol was completely bare except for a tiny pot-bellied stove that gave off a fitful warmth and just enough light to pick out objects close by. A pile of coal lay next to it directly on the dirt floor—no box, no scuttle, nothing. Beside that was a crockery bowl and a spoon. Empty.

"Is everyone all right?" he said hoarsely, getting his knees under him, and then his feet. Water ran off his face in runnels. "Oscar?"

"Well enough." The corporal was still breathing heavily. "Where is it?"

"Davey has it."

A long exhalation of breath. "Thank you. They took everything when they searched me. Emptied my pouches, took my knife. I can bear those losses if I know it is safe."

"If what is safe?" came a rasping voice out of a dark corner.

William could swear his heart stopped.

Victoria
5:20 p.m.

The rain pounded so loudly on the roof of the boarding house that Daisy could barely hear Freddie speak.

"What was that, dearest?" *Oh, William. Are you safe and dry in this deluge? How can we find you?*

"I said, we must travel light. Our Colts and harness, warm jackets, boots, and a rucksack of food."

"In other words, our standard equipment when going for a stroll in town?"

"Exactly. I wish we still had Davey's bombs." Her sister's voice was grim in the lamplit room. "I should take great satisfaction in bombing Pig Iron Kelly's vessel to oblivion."

"I only hope that our dear ones are not aboard it. A man like him would use them for insurance against just such a possibility, don't you think?"

"Good point," Freddie said. Downstairs, the gong rang. "I do not feel much like eating, but since Papa refuses to lift in this storm, I suppose we must go down to dinner."

"You know our philosophy."

"I do. I expect Papa has adopted the same in his travels, too. We are not expected to dress, are we?"

"I hardly think so," Daisy said. "We are the only guests here, and Jake does not strike me as the kind of man to be impressed by lace and *décolletage*. If one possessed either."

Freddie made a sound that was almost a giggle. Almost.

They sat down to a dinner that was both nourishing and plentiful. If she had not been so fearful and distressed about their friends, Daisy would have been awestruck at the repast Mrs Birch and her cook provided for them. Pork chops in raisin and apple sauce, beet greens with beets chopped fine and sprinkled with walnuts, and for dessert, a ginger cake with caramel frosting.

"My compliments on the finest meal I have enjoyed in a year," Papa said over his glass of port. "A work of art from beginning to end, Madame."

Mrs Birch blushed at the praise. "I do have a reputation to uphold," she said modestly. "I am very glad you enjoyed it. Young Mr Harrow is in training here—you may thank him for the whole."

A young man leaned in the door just long enough to receive their thanks before he disappeared again, and the clinking of cutlery and china commenced in the sink.

"He aspires to join the staff at the Empress," Mrs Birch explained, "but he must have experience first. He is the son of my next-door neighbor, and is a dear boy. He will do well."

"May we beg provisions for tomorrow, Mrs Birch?" Daisy asked. "Since we do not know when we will return, we must plan to take food with us."

"Of course, dear," the lady said, waving a hand as though this were the least she could do. "Did I not say? Mr Harrow, who is a wizard with pastry, has made enough pork and onion pasties for two days, with three extra for your friends, who will no doubt need sustenance on the return journey. I have dried apples from the orchard, water in canteens, and—" She lowered her voice. "The last half of that cake is to go with you as well."

"You are an angel," Papa said. "We cannot express enough gratitude for your care and foresight."

The blush deepened. "I must confess that you are not my

first guests whose loved ones have fallen into the hands of the pirates. I outfitted them in just this way."

"And did they return successful?" Jake asked, forking up the last of his second piece of cake.

Mrs Birch looked crestfallen. "Sadly, no. We had reports that they were all killed. But at least they went well prepared."

Oh, dear. Daisy exchanged a despairing glance with her sister.

Both of them held out their plates for another piece of cake.

CHAPTER 8

WHITBY ISLAND

6:30 p.m.

"I am Annie," the voice whispered. "Annie Fowler. Who are you?"

A young woman—probably about Daisy's age—crept into the tiny pool of light cast by the isinglass window set in the door of the stove. Her eyes appeared huge because of the bruises, and her face was thin, her hair so lank it almost looked wet.

William's heart swelled with pity. "I am William Barnicott. My ward Davey Fletcher is with me. And Corporal Kent of the RCAP."

An intake of breath. "Not the inspector's son?"

"Indeed," said the corporal after a slight pause. "Our ship was shot down. Miles from here. Where the sound gives on to the channel."

"What did you do wrong?" Davey had recovered enough to speak. "Will they feed us?"

"Yes, eventually," Annie said with a glance at the empty

bowl, her voice a little stronger. "And I did nothing wrong. I was simply in the wrong place at the wrong time. Our steamship docked here in error. Half of us were on the pier before the captain realized his mistake." She sighed. "I did not run fast enough."

Steamships docked here? "How long ago was that?" William asked.

"I cannot tell," she confessed. "Thirteen days, perhaps? Fifteen? I have lost track."

"You've been locked in here for *two weeks*?" Davey asked.

"They take me out now and again. For amusement."

Dear heaven. "Will no one miss you?" Oscar asked. "Surely assistance must be on its way."

The girl was silent. A silence filled with the lash of rain on the door. "I—I have no one of whom to demand a ransom," she said at last. "They have questioned me repeatedly, but I cannot give an answer I do not have. It is a punishable offense." Her voice trailed away.

A spark of rage lit in William's gut. "They will regret that, I promise you."

"I hope for your sakes that you *do* have an answer," she said, her gaze moving from one to the next. "A name."

"I shall not give it," Oscar said bluntly.

"Are you in uniform?" she asked. "I apologize that I cannot see you properly—my spectacles were broken."

"No apology necessary, Miss Fowler. And yes, I am in uniform."

"Then they already know. A pigeon is probably already in the air."

"The RCAP does not give in to the demands of pirates," Oscar snapped.

"But your father, surely—"

"How do you know about his father?" Davey wanted to know. "You knew his name straight off."

A movement of air, as though she chuckled but did not have the strength to make it any stronger. "Everyone in these islands knows his name," she said. "Inspector Kent is Pig Iron Kelly's worst enemy. He is probably already drunk on his triumph at capturing you, sir."

"He will enjoy his whiskey more than anything he will get from the RCAP," Oscar said grimly.

"In that case, I feel sorry for you," she said sadly. "You appear a noble sort of person. It is a shame …" Her voice trailed away. "What about you, Mr Barnicott? Do you have reason to hope?"

"I trust in love and family, not money," William said, managing to straighten his aching back. Where the RCAP had failed, Daisy would not. Somehow, during this hellish day, that thought had kept him going. The Linden sisters had faced worse than this and emerged triumphant. A few air pirates would not stop their coming to the aid of their little party.

"Then you are a fool," Annie said bitterly. "Your family are doomed if they try a rescue. Truly, your chances are better with a ransom. Kelly is diabolical, but he has his own code. He does not harm children very much, and if he receives the ransom he demands, he does set the prisoner free."

"I find that difficult to believe," Oscar said.

"The last one was several days ago. I think. I started to count the days, but then got confused. In any case, they were talking about it around the fire. They seemed to consider it a great joke that the man was freed, and during the rescue, they seized two of the steamship crew that came to deliver the money." A pause. "They were released a couple of days past, but I have not heard if they escaped the islands altogether. I have learned there are pirate airfields on seven of these islands. Escape is a matter of luck, I think."

"You don't paint a very hopeful picture," William said.

"Set them free, only to capture the people who come for them?" Davey's voice was scornful. "Dirty trick, I'd say."

"But at least there is hope," she said faintly. "Some must escape. And some, like me ..." Again, her voice trailed away.

William could not imagine the girl's fate. From the stories he had heard, it was too horrible to contemplate. "We cannot allow it," he said fiercely. "We have the means to ransom you, too, Miss Fowler. You must not give up."

"You do?" she said, the faintest note of hope in her voice.

"We have an ingot of Californio gold," Davey told her proudly.

"Davey!" both he and Oscar barked simultaneously.

It was their most closely held secret. That ingot was to finance their future in Victoria, not to be handed over to flea-infested pirates to drink its weight in whiskey. William had thought to ask Daisy to sell her engagement ring for the ransom. The Viceroy's ruby would fetch a price that would make even a pirate sit up and take notice. And Daisy would surrender it instantly if it meant their being together again.

"Well, we do," the boy said defensively. "We tell the pirates, Daisy and Freddie bring it, and we go free. All four of us. Miss Fowler can find employment in Victoria, I'm sure, and take up her life again. Just like us."

"You must not speak of things you know nothing about. Not to anyone," William said harshly. "Miss Fowler, I beg you, forget what this rash young man has just said."

"But I didn't mean to— I only wanted to—" Davey began to sniffle. William had never spoken to him in such a tone before.

"Of course not," she said softly. "Davey, don't cry. My lips are sealed."

"We have other means," William said, not quite ready yet to forgive the boy's stupidity in confessing their secret to a complete stranger, no matter how desperate her plight. "When they come, we will give the pirates a name, and there will be an end to it."

"Thank you for listening to me," she whispered. "A man a few days back would not, and they—they—well, I heard his screams." She choked and could say no more.

William decided that was a good place to leave the conversation for Davey to think on. He got up and moved cautiously over to the door, tried the handle, then made a circuit of the room. His examination did not take long. He joined his fellow prisoners huddled around the stove.

"No furniture or firewood to use for a club. Only the coal, for which I am grateful, but it is no weapon. Miss Fowler, have you no possessions?"

"They took my valise and my reticule, which contained my identification papers and my money," she said sadly. "And my grandmother's embroidered handkerchief, my only memento of her."

"We have nothing to do but wait," Oscar said, "and hope that the little heat we have will dry our clothes by morning. I am certainly not removing anything with a lady present."

"I am willing to donate a petticoat as a towel, if it will help," Annie said.

"Indeed not. We will huddle together and do our best to wait out the night."

"Waiting is the worst," she said on a sad note. "I hope that—"

The door crashed open and William slammed his eyelids shut against the lancing pain of the moonglobes' glare.

"You! Woman!" someone shouted. "Out here, now. We want a good time!"

Annie made a pathetic sound and her skirts whispered as she moved to obey. William opened his eyes at a scrape of furious movement, and squinted as Oscar flung himself in front of her. "No!"

A club swung out of the dark, held by someone who was only a silhouette.

Oscar collapsed.

The door slammed shut and the dark fell like a curtain.

"I hate this place!" Davey wailed, and would have begun to cry in earnest had not William seized him roughly in his arms and given him a bear hug.

"I hate this place, too," he said, willing his eyes to adjust so that he could examine Oscar. "Forgive me for being so angry. But now, we must help Oscar. All right? We must do our best to survive. Together. No matter what. Do you understand?"

"Yes," Davey said, muffled against his coat. "No matter what."

Together, they knelt beside their friend.

Victoria
January 15, 1896
12:10 a.m.

FREDDIE WOKE with a start to the sound of pounding on the front door. A moment later, Jake's door opened and she heard the creak of his footsteps as he slipped down the stairs. A second, heavier set followed from the next room. Papa.

"News of William!" The lamp on the table between their two beds flared to life as Daisy lit it. Then she flung her shawl about her shoulders. "Come, Freddie."

Freddie snatched up her own shawl and they tiptoed down the stairs with the lamp to come up short next to the newel post. Mrs Birch stood in her bedroom doorway, tying the sash of her embroidered wrapper while Jake stood aside to admit Inspector Kent. She had never pictured the man in civilian clothes. It was strange to think he even possessed any. His shirt had been stuffed into a pair of denim trousers such as cowboys wore, and a plaid wool coat pulled on in such haste one side of the collar was rolled under.

"Marcus," Mrs Birch said, crossing the little vestibule to fix the collar, "what has happened?"

"A ransom demand has arrived."

Daisy made a high sound in her throat and her knees gave out. She was barely able to retain hold of the lamp. Papa slipped an arm about her and guided her into the sitting room. Freddie and the others followed, and Mrs Birch powered the electricks into a dim glow while Jake stirred up the fire and put two pieces of wood on it.

"Tell us," Daisy croaked.

"It came by pigeon a few minutes ago, addressed to me.

But it is clear that Pig Iron Kelly believes us to be acquainted." He unfolded a piece of paper of a much better quality than Freddie would have expected. Probably stolen.

Kent,

Your son Oscar and two fellows, William Barnicott and Davey, are in my custody, charged with murder, criminal trespass, threat to kill, and wrecking. The penalty for these crimes is death. However, I am willing to commute their sentences in exchange for a suitable contribution to the well-being of the communities in my charge. I understand you or persons known to you are in possession of Californio gold—

Daisy gasped. Freddie's cheeks went cold as the blood drained out of them. Inspector Kent's lashes flicked up, as though they had interrupted him, before he went on.

—which I require as earnest for their safe return. We will expect you by noon tomorrow, regardless of weather, at the village at the head of the sound on Whitby Island. Come alone. Any sign of RCAP interference in these negotiations will be understood as an attack upon our citizens, and an appropriate defense mounted without delay.

Your servant,

Poulson Isaiah Kelly, Esq.

"How—?" Daisy choked on a sob. "How could they possibly have told him?"

"Told him what?" Inspector Kent said with exaggerated patience.

"About the gold ingot!" she wailed. "Have they been

tortured? Maimed? Oh, what have our friends been through that in their extremity they would give up such a secret?"

"A gold ingot?" Jake said with interest. "Truly? How did you come by that?"

"Honestly, I assure y—" Freddie got out before Inspector Kent made a slashing movement with his hand.

"It is irrelevant," he snapped. "Gold or no gold, we do not negotiate with pirates."

"You may not, but we do," Papa said with some heat. "We shall take the ingot to them."

"If you attempt to lift, you will be arrested and tossed in gaol, and believe me, you will not have such an easy time as you did in Port Townsend," Inspector Kent said through his teeth. "You are grounded, do you understand me?"

"How can you say that?" Freddie demanded. "We are talking about *your son!*"

Daisy's mouth trembled but her eyes were snapping with anger. "If they have been tortured to give up knowledge of that ingot, their sacrifice shall *not* be in vain."

Behind Inspector Kent, gliding through an oval portrait on the wall, came a misty figure. Female. Hair piled on top of her head and held in place by a bandeau, her traveling costume of a fashion popular a decade ago. As the figure paused in front of the window and the clouds parted to allow a glimmer of moonlight, Freddie realized that the bandeau was not decorative at all—it was a pair of flying goggles.

She drew a long breath. Her gaze went to the portrait on the wall beside the fire, which she'd paid no attention to earlier.

Clementine Birch Kent.

The figure turned, put her hands upon slender hips, and glared at her husband.

"Mrs Kent would be ashamed of you," came out of Freddie's mouth before she could stop the words.

"What did you say?" The inspector took a step toward her, but Jake slid smoothly between them.

"Deep breaths, Inspector," he said pleasantly. "We must stay calm."

"If you persist in telling me what to do, young man, I shall have you detained for obstruction," he snapped. Then his glare practically burned Freddie's face. "I asked you, Frederica, to repeat what you said to me."

"I merely stated the obvious." Freddie locked her knees and laid one hand on the back of the chair to hold herself up under the blast of his rage. "Mrs Kent would be ashamed of such a stance—as would any woman, mother or not, whose loved ones were in danger."

In the window, Clementine gave a decided nod, and folded her arms over her chest.

"I—I have somewhat of a reputation as a medium," Freddie went on while both Daisy and Papa lost their color at hearing it spoken aloud. "I woke from a dream of her just now, dressed in a traveling costume, a pair of flying goggles pushed up in her hair."

Now it was Inspector Kent's turn to turn pale. In fact, the only person in the room not white as bleached linen was Jake, who kept a watch on the inspector in case he should make any sudden movements.

For which she was grateful.

"A traveling costume?" the inspector croaked.

"Yes, trimmed with—" She glanced at the misty figure in

the window. Bother. No colors were manifested. "Her blouse was trimmed with lace at the throat, and the jacket was belted."

Inspector Kent sat in the armchair rather suddenly.

Clementine bent toward him as though to assure herself that he was all right.

"It is what she was wearing when we—when she—"

"Do not distress yourself, Inspector." Freddie plucked up her courage and crossed the room to kneel by his chair. "She is always with you, her love and courage so strong that I believe she defies even the laws of nature to remain with you. Watching out for you and Oscar. So you must believe me when I say that she would want you to put rules and regulations aside and act from your heart."

"But I cannot abandon my post." Some stony barrier that had held his emotions back deep inside seemed to shiver and crack. Freddie saw a bright sliver of the agony that was burning him up inside. "My son!" he said in a hoarse whisper. "I cannot lose him, too. Neither can I leave my men when we could be attacked."

"Of course not," she said. "The men need their commander. You have no ships that will arrive by tomorrow at noon in any case. You are grounded, sir, and not by choice. That is why you must let us go to Oscar's aid. Well armed and outfitted, mind you, and with your blessing and support."

"But you—mere civilians—women—"

Jake chuckled. "I would not finish that sentence if I were you, Inspector. The bravest, most accomplished fighters and strategists I know are women. I would put my life in the hands of any one of them with complete confidence."

Clementine tilted her chin imperiously as though to include herself in that number.

"She was a woman like that, was your wife," Freddie said to Inspector Kent. "You must honor her and, with her blessing, send us in your stead."

Kent's grip on Freddie's shoulder was almost painful as the barrier split and was washed away in the tears that spilled from his eyes. "I cannot bear it," he whispered. "I cannot bear the thought of losing him. I have pushed him away, treated him as though he were at fault. I cannot live with myself now —how could I bear life then?"

"You will not have to," Freddie said, aware that Clementine had rushed straight through the sofa and was kneeling on her husband's other side, a ghostly hand touching his face. Offering comfort. Offering forgiveness. "Clementine knows you love him. That you no longer blame him for her death."

"You speak … almost as if she were here," he said in wonder. "And yet it was only a dream."

"Love is not a dream," Freddie said with fierce certainty. "Love is as real as you or I, and with us at this moment."

Clementine kissed him with fierce passion, and for a moment his gaze lost its focus, as though he had been reminded of a similar kiss long ago.

"You are right," he said, and wiped away his tears with the flat of his hand. Not as though he were ashamed of them, but in the manner of a man putting aside the past to look into the future. "You shall go with my blessing and all the support you need from the RCAP."

"Bombs?" Jake said hopefully.

Freddie nearly smiled. Davey would have said exactly the same thing.

"I might be able to requisition a bomb or two," Inspector Kent allowed. "But to be used only as a last resort. There are prisoners and civilians on those islands, too."

"In any case," Papa said, "the conveyance will not bear the weight of too many armaments. I believe we will be better served by our wits and our courage."

"You have no shortage of that in your family," Inspector Kent said, looking down into Freddie's face.

She smiled up at him. A person might just come to love such a man as a father-in-law.

After she reconciled herself to having a ghost for a mother-in-law.

CHAPTER 9

5:50 a.m.

*D*aisy would never have thought that after such a harrowing midnight hour—including what amounted to Freddie's revelation to a near stranger of her peculiar ability—that the two of them would have been able to sleep. But some dreadful tension had been broken. Or perhaps it was the breaking of a strong man's guilt that had caused this sense of freedom in the household.

Downstairs, she could hear Mrs Birch singing as she and young Mr Harrow prepared breakfast. The smell of excellent coffee wafted up the stairwell. The inspector was to present himself at the table at seven o'clock, a fact that had made Papa grumble last night. He was still not reconciled to Freddie's revealing her own most closely guarded secret, and Daisy was sure he meant to prevent any further hints.

She and her sister dressed carefully in the split skirts they had bought in Reno and never expected to wear in public. They were made of soft buckskin and fell to the ankles, revealing the buckles and laces of their boots, but only just. Chambray shirts and warm, fitted wool jackets went overtop, and the effect was finished with their gun harnesses slung about their hips.

Jake met them on the landing, his eyebrows rising as he took them in. "There was a time when I'd have called this your raiding rig."

Daisy smiled in delight. "I feel a little as though I am going raiding. Or rescuing, anyway, which may amount to the same thing before this day is over."

Papa found them in the kitchen, packing a tin case with the pork and onion pasties, dried apples, and water canteens Mrs Birch had promised them yesterday. "My girls, I have been thinking," he said.

On what subject had Papa applied his fearsome intellect? "Of that I have no doubt," Daisy said.

"In one respect I agree with our friend the inspector. I have concluded that you cannot simply hand over the ingot to pirates."

Daisy felt as though her father had dealt her a blow to the stomach.

Mrs Birch stopped her cheery humming of "Daisy Bell" in mid-note and turned from the bacon and eggs sizzling merrily in the cast-iron frying pan. "Are their lives not worth its value?" Shock seemed to have reduced her vocabulary to the barest minimum.

Her father frowned at Mrs Birch and then Daisy as though they had answered *five* to his request for the product of two times two. "Of course they are. That was never in question. But can we not provide a convincing substitute? Why should we hand over the real thing when it is meant to sustain and establish our family?"

Daisy stared at him. Where did one find a convincing substitute for a solid gold ingot in—she glanced at the caseless chronometer on the windowsill—five and a half hours, less flight time?

"I have to say I have been turning that same question over in my mind," Jake said. He seemed to be watching the breakfast preparations with interest, but Daisy had the impression his thoughts were engaged elsewhere, like the many wheels and gears of a difference engine. "But how can we create a substitute in a couple of hours, short of gold-plating a bar of lead?"

"Gold is heavier than lead," Freddie said, having clearly retained Papa's natural science lessons from childhood much better than Daisy had.

"What are the odds the pirates have a scale?" Jake riposted with a grin.

Papa's gaze lay on Jake with gratified approval. "You have hit it on the head," he said. "We shall gold plate a casing of iron filled with lead. The iron will protect the lead from the heat, so that it will not melt while we apply the gold."

"Where are we doing this?" Jake said, half laughing, as though he believed Papa to be making a joke. "Here in the kitchen?"

"Not *my* kitchen," Mrs Birch said firmly, and dished up the food. A knock sounded on the door. "Daisy, if you will put this basket of biscuits and these two jars of plum jam on the table, Freddie can let Marcus in. He is just in time."

But Papa was not finished with the problem. He barely allowed Inspector Kent to get started on his breakfast before he presented their thinking to him. "We cannot melt gold here, though Mrs Birch's cast-iron pan would do the job in a pinch. Do you have another suggestion?"

"You need a forge," Inspector Kent said.

"You need Capital Iron Works, then, on Store Street," Mrs Birch said promptly. "Maurice Greenaway is the blacksmith. He is the only man in town with the skill to do such a thing."

"Why would he help us?" Papa asked. "We are about to demand a miracle."

"I introduced him to his wife," Mrs Birch said rather smugly. "He will do anything I ask."

8:00 a.m.

Half an hour after finishing breakfast, they presented themselves at the large, half-timbered building, where the lower floor gave on the harbor so that steamships might dock for repair, and the upper opened on the street. Mrs Birch explained their problem with efficiency, and the smith's brows rose almost into his bushy hair.

"Ye dinna ask much, do ye?" he said, eyeing the ingot they laid upon his bench. "Aye, I can fill an iron mold wi' lead and melt a bit o' yer gold to cover it, but I canna guarantee it will hold together. To reverse the polarity and make the gold adhere, I need an electric charge more powerful than the sorry electricks we have hereabouts."

Jake pulled a rather terrifying looking weapon from his belt. "I believe this will do, sir."

The man's eyes widened. "I have heard tell o' such things, but never thought to see one."

"If you do your part, the lightning pistol will do the rest."

96

Whitby Island
8:56 a.m.

Annie Fowler had not come back.

William, Davey, and Oscar had spent a damp, wakeful night on the floor of the gaol, as close to the potbellied stove as they could come without being burned. Every sound dragged William out of sleep in case it was she, and he would be forced to use his doctoring skills and perhaps even the previously offered petticoat to bind up her wounds. The only evidence they had that a new day had dawned was the brief opening of the door, which let in a vertical glow of light.

Someone shoved a small copper pot inside before it was slammed and locked once more.

"Porridge," Davey reported, peering in at the contents. "But they didn't give us any spoons."

"We have hands," William told him. "Let us use them in case this is all we are given today."

"They took my chocolate," the boy mourned as he dipped his fingers into the gluey, nearly cold mass. "I'd rather have that."

"I'd rather eat raw oysters, myself," Oscar told him. "My sisters love porridge, with brown sugar and raisins and chopped apples, and inflict it upon their children regularly. But prisoners can't be choosers."

William did his best to imagine the porridge full of sweetmeats, choking it down and then, when it was gone, licking his fingers clean. The fingers added an aftertaste of oyster and cedar needles and dirt, but at least his stomach was less empty than it had been.

"Do you think we can use that pot as a weapon on the next

person who comes in?" Davey asked, following William's example and sucking his fingers clean.

"We can try," Oscar said. "It is unlikely they would have given it to us if it could be used as an actual weapon. One blow would probably damage the pot more than someone's head, but I will not waste a chance to use it."

Victoria
10:50 a.m.

Mrs Birch had chivvied the party back to the boarding house, leaving Jake and Inspector Kent to guard the ingot and participate in the process. Midmorning saw the conveyance prepared for travel—and armed as well as it could be given that it had been designed for healing, not for battle.

"I cannot bear it," Daisy said at last. "I must go back to Capital Iron Works to see if Mr Greenaway has been success-ful. It is nearly eleven. We are running out of time."

"We can save half an hour of walking if we simply take the conveyance," Freddie suggested. "I have already put in Jake's coat and the rucksack. We can put down on the pier. Plenty of bollards there to moor to."

Daisy hugged her. "You are brilliant." Then she kissed Mrs Birch. "Thank you for all your help. We will be back by sunset."

"I know you will," their hostess said softly. She took Papa's hand. "Good luck."

He looked rather as though he might offer her a kiss, too, but did not. Even so, Mrs Birch blushed and released his hand as though just realizing she still held it.

Papa climbed into the pilot's chair, Freddie on to the rear

bench, and when Daisy had the boiler up to full steam, he called, "Up ship!" Young Mr Harrow released the ropes. They floated up over the apple trees and made a tight turn for the waterfront.

In only five minutes, Papa set the vanes to vertical for the short approach to the pier. It was the work of a moment to tie the conveyance down, and then they were running for the forge. They fell through the door just in time to see a blast of lightning arc out from Jake's pistol, which he held steady with both hands. Its target was an open tank of water in which a gold ingot was suspended. The suspension material lasted but a moment before it was burned away, and the lightning flickered through the water, exploring the surface of the ingot with hot blue and white tendrils, lovingly enveloping it and then dissipating. The ingot dropped through the liquid to the floor of the tank with a clang.

"My word," Freddie breathed in Daisy's ear. "You don't suppose he would use that pistol on a human being, do you?"

"I haven't the courage to ask," Daisy whispered back.

Mr Greenaway reached into the tank with a pair of muffled tongs, removed the ingot, and ran the back of his hand over it to test its temperature. Then he presented the ingot to Inspector Kent. "That should do it. Dinna be afraid to take it. It's quite cool."

Kent took it in his hands and turned it over. "It looks and feels exactly like the original," he said in wonder. He handed it to Papa, who gave it to Daisy for examination.

"Well done," Papa said, and offered the smith his hand. "I hope you have taken a bit from said original as your fee."

"Nay." The big man shook his head. "A paltry bit of gold like that can never pay for these years of happiness. I owe Mrs

Birch much more. Besides, not every man has the opportunity to see a lightning pistol. I only hope you will return successful." He glanced at Inspector Kent, who took the hint.

"You must go," he said to the Lindens. "I will see the original ingot to headquarters, where it will be locked in my safe until you return to claim it."

"And this," Jake said, handing the pistol to Kent. "Should something go wrong, it can't fall into the hands of the pirates."

Daisy wrapped the false ingot in a bit of cloth, where she was obliged to hold it from the bottom so its weight did not reveal its presence to any passer-by on the dock. They wasted no time preparing the conveyance, so that within moments, their brave, hopeful little party was in the air. They had half an hour to cross the strait and reach the rendezvous point.

Whitby Island
11:40 a.m.

Their chance to escape came at nearly midday with the thump of footsteps outside. Oscar leaped to his feet and swept up the copper porridge pot in one hand, stationing himself beside the door moments before it was flung open.

"All right, you lot—"

The pot came down on the pirate's head with all the force of which Oscar was capable. The pirate cried out and stumbled forward, where William ambushed him with a kick to the stomach and an elbow to the head. Oscar was able strike the next pirate, too, before three more burst in and laid him out with a punch. The pot hit the floor with a clang and rolled into the corner, where Davey pounced on it and whirled, ready to use it.

Bang!

The gunshot brought the fracas to an abrupt end. Two revolvers were leveled at William and the unmoving Oscar, and the man with the club advanced on Davey with a growl. But Davey met him step for step, and it wasn't until the club came down and smashed the copper pot from his hands that he howled and was forced to retreat behind William.

"Davey—" he began. How many of the boy's fingers had just been broken?

"Shut up! Enough of this nonsense," the man with the club said. "You're to come with us."

"Where?" William demanded.

Oscar struggled up from the floor. William's relief found expression in a long exhalation of breath. For a few dreadful moments he had thought the corporal's skull might have been fractured.

"Shut up! You'll see soon enough."

They were herded out the door and down the path. In the daylight, William could now see how isolated the gaol was, built into its hillside a hundred yards or so outside the village proper. There were actual streets, with neat frame houses painted white or grey, and fruit trees whose size and age hinted at many harvests. Surely the village could not have been built by these men—slovenly and violent and reeking of homemade liquor. It was far more likely that the pirates had attacked the original inhabitants and either forced them into servitude, driven them out, or killed them.

The streets led down to the shore that formed the head of the long inlet. In a large field, three grey airships were moored. There was room for at least six. How many were in Pig Iron's fleet? William wondered. Were there similar villages and airfields of this size scattered throughout these islands, as Annie had said, kept in constant communication by pigeon?

Where *was* Annie, that poor woman? Had the "entertainment" last night been the end of her?

And what did the pirates want with them now? For the storm had cleared away, the last clouds racing south to reveal a clean-washed sky. The sun was high, too, its rays piercing the forest to lie upon his bruised face like the kind hand of a friend.

He reached over to examine Davey's hands and was jabbed in the back by a rifle stock for his pains.

A man disembarked from the middle ship and advanced toward them with a woman pressed against his side. She was well dressed in a pale blue walking costume, her blond hair curled and braided in a coronet. William blinked and focused, and the bottom fell out of his stomach.

Annie.

She was smiling and looking up at the man. Could this be Pig Iron Kelly? William had expected a giant, with beefy arms and a black beard, like Sarge. Instead, he saw a tall, clean-shaven individual in an immaculate black coat, with white lace at collar and cuffs. His boots gleamed with buckles, and his grey wool trousers were not defiled with mud. He walked with a slight limp. If not for the aeronaut's goggles pushed up on his head, he would look for all the world like a professor of English William had once had as a tutor at Harvard, years ago, back when he was a freshman and believed that an education would make the world his apple.

Professor—oh, what had his name been—

William sucked in a breath so fast he choked on it.

The pirates stepped away, leaving William and his two companions exposed to view.

"You all right, Annie?" Davey asked anxiously.

She might be respectably dressed, but she didn't appear to be bruised. Perhaps these men gave their beatings on parts that could not be seen.

"Mrs Kelly to you," the man said pleasantly.

William felt as though he were that copper pot, ringing like a gong as it hit the floor. He glared at Annie. "So it was all a lie?" he rasped. "About the steamship, and the beatings? All of it?"

"No," she said. "I did arrive on a steamship. But I found that my prospects were better here than they ever would have been in Victoria. Especially when I met my husband." She smiled up at him, and for the life of him, William thought it looked real.

"It's Professor Poulson Kelly, isn't it?" William said. "Faculty of Humanities, Harvard?"

The man looked astonished. "Good heavens. I haven't heard that address in a lifetime. Do I know you?"

"You were my tutor. William Barnicott. Chemistry major. English failure."

The man's eyes filled with humor. "The chemistry building. I remember now."

William inclined his head. "I was expelled, ending our lessons together. But how did you come to be here?"

"I was expelled, too, but not for the same reason. It is a tale which, sadly, I will not be sharing with you. For your ransom will arrive shortly and there simply isn't time to do the whole story justice."

"Our … ransom?" Oscar was the only one with the courage to ask, the astonishment plain in his tone.

"Yes. Your lives are quite valuable, I understand, Mr Barnicott." He bowed to Oscar, who was barely able to stay on his feet. "But you, Corporal, are worth far more. I'm sure that our ingot of Californio gold is entirely down to you, and no one else."

In a single moment, the pieces all fell into place in William's dazed brain. Their confidences of last night with a woman they believed to have been a prisoner. Davey's mistake.

"You didn't," he breathed.

"Would not you have?" Kelly inquired, as though they were talking about a hand of cards. "One tiny slip of a stupid boy's tongue, and not only do I have a name, I have quite the treasure, too. Honestly, it is I who should be thanking you."

"They'll never give it to you," Davey told him fiercely, as though he might make amends simply by saying the words.

"It means our future," William added, knowing his own protest was futile.

"It certainly does," Kelly agreed. "For if I do not see a delivery by the stroke of noon, my men here will form a firing squad. Though," he said thoughtfully, eyeing William, "I remember quite liking you. Do you remember the formula you used to blow up that building?"

"It was an accident," William said through his teeth. "How can I be expected to remember a mistake? The vial was unlabeled—I didn't know it was nitric acid."

"If Inspector Kent does maintain his habit of ignoring my demands, perhaps I might make you an offer. A man who can blow up a building by accident might be very useful if he were to attempt it on purpose."

"I will do no such thing," William snapped.

Kelly shrugged. "Suit yourself." He pulled a gold watch on a chain from the pocket of his brocade waistcoat. "You have five minutes in which to change your mind."

CHAPTER 10

WHITBY ISLAND

Noon

Their course from Victoria to the village on Whitby was essentially a straight line, but Jake and Papa did not trust that there would not be men with rifles stationed on the rise of ground to the southwest. With Jake and his lightning pistol ready at the viewing port, Papa brought the conveyance around by the northeast, giving Daisy a full view of the wreckage of poor downed Number Thirteen, its fuselage snagged in the tall pines, its gondola hanging down the cliff face almost on the vertical.

They completed their turn and Papa brought the conveyance in on a long approach, straight up the inlet. Waiting for them at the airfield at the foot of the village was a half-circle of men, and at its head were three familiar figures.

"All ready for us, I see," Jake remarked.

Tears welled up in Daisy's eyes and spilled over. She hadn't meant to cry. She meant to be a rock for William, who had no doubt been through agonies he would never confess to her.

But merely the sight of his posture in the distance was enough to burst her control like a dam.

She had her face mopped up by the time they landed, and told herself sternly she must not give these miscreants the opportunity to see her break down again. But Papa had other ideas.

"Daisy, you will stay with the conveyance," he said grimly as he set it down some fifty feet away with hardly a bump. Two boys ran to loop the ropes over mooring irons. "Keep the boiler at full steam, for we will have a very quick departure once our friends are aboard."

"But Papa—"

"I will have no argument. You and Freddie are too vulnerable here."

"We are fully armed, Papa," Daisy said indignantly.

"And Clementine is not the only woman who can shoot a wolf in the eye at twenty yards." Freddie's body was rigid, watching Corporal Kent's clearly injured form through the viewing port as though her will alone could keep him upright.

Papa was having none of it. "Jake and I will go and make the exchange. Daisy, cover us with your Colt. Have that little Thaxton at hand in case we are forced to fight at close quarters. Freddie, tend the boiler. Full steam, mind."

Daisy had a wild moment to wonder what Aunt Jane would think of such instructions from her studious, unassuming brother-in-law, and bit back a hysterical urge to laugh.

She pulled the Colt from its holster as Freddie handed the false ingot to Papa and he climbed down. Even though she had already inspected it before they left, Daisy pulled the hammer back, opened the load gate, and spun the cylinder to make certain all six cartridges were ready to fire. With the load gate closed once more, she pulled the hammer back the rest of the way, pulled the trigger lightly, then eased the hammer forward.

The Thaxton lay in her pocket, its two shots loaded and simpler to manage. Taking up a position at the bow of the conveyance, she propped both arms on one of the furled vanes and took aim.

Papa paced across the field with unconscious dignity, Jake at his side, and paused about thirty feet from the assembly. "I have the ransom," he said clearly. "You may release my friends."

"No!" Davey broke free and ran across the grass. "Don't give it to them, Professor! Don't!"

Papa regarded him solemnly. "I must. Run to the conveyance and prepare to lift."

"No—please—I never meant—I didn't know she was his wife!"

"Do as you're told, Davey," Jake bit off.

Davey choked back a wail and ran for the conveyance. Daisy did not move the Colt, in case someone gave chase, but he reached them without incident. "Get inside, Davey," she said.

"I didn't mean to tell!"

"I know you didn't." She would not permit him to believe this was his fault. "Get inside. We will lift as soon as William and Oscar are secured."

"You'd better. They catch the people who bring the ransom, and demand ransom for them."

"We are ready," she said, her gaze never leaving her father.

A well-dressed man limped toward him, and bowed courteously before he took the false ingot. He unwrapped the tea towel and regarded its gleaming, heavy contents with delight. Then he made a motion over his shoulder. Someone gave William a push in the small of his back. He stumbled forward, clutching at Oscar, and together they half-ran, half-walked toward Papa.

The well-dressed pirate—it had to be Pig Iron Kelly—walked slowly away, the ingot cradled in his hands like a baby rabbit. Jake threw an arm around Oscar from the other side, and between he and William, Oscar's feet hardly touched the grass as they covered the ground to the conveyance under the watchful eye of Daisy's Colt.

"Ropes," Papa said to Daisy as he wrenched open the rear door and they bundled Oscar inside. "Freddie, up ship!"

Jake released the aft rope while Daisy cast off the bow line. Then they leaped inside as the conveyance left the ground. Daisy pulled William into her embrace, hard. She would never let him out of her sight again. Propriety could go straight to perdition.

Papa made a tight turn and opened up the engine while at the firebox, Freddie laid on coal like a madwoman. In moments they were out of range of even a cannon, on a course straight down the sound. Once they were over open water and beginning their climb into the blessed sky, Daisy's lungs remembered how to expand again.

"Darling," she whispered, taking William's poor abused face gently between her hands. He had a black eye, and a trickle of blood had dried at the corner of his mouth. "How badly have they hurt you?"

"Nothing that won't heal," he panted, still out of breath after the awkward gallop across the field. "I have tinctures and herbs in back to make poultices for both of us. And I must examine Davey's hands. I fear his fingers may be broken."

Daisy made a sound of distress, and touched him here, there—cataloguing jaw, shoulder, arms, chest. She must make certain each one still operated. Then with infinite gentleness, she kissed him, butterfly light, upon his poor mouth. "How you must have suffered. We have been in agonies, too … of a different kind. And Corporal Kent? Is he injured?"

"I am perfectly well," came on a groan from the rear bench, where the corporal lay on his side, his knees brought up to his chest.

Her labors with the engine temporarily completed, Freddie hung over the the bench from the engine compartment. "We are going as fast as we can," she assured him. "We will have you in sick bay at headquarters within the hour."

He turned himself slowly on to his back so that he could gaze up at her. "The sight of you is all the medicine I need."

"You are delirious, poor man. But is anything broken?" Freddie asked, leaning closer as though she might see for herself.

"I do not think so," he croaked. "I believe I am concussed."

"They laid him out," William said. "We took down two of them, however, before the gunfire began."

Daisy shuddered.

"We will fly directly to Victoria once I make this turn past the point," Papa reported.

At his words, Daisy felt some of the terrible tension leaching from his body. "We learned that there are seven pirate villages, likely with airships stationed in each. The wonder of it is that Victoria has not been attacked already."

"We have our own fleet," Oscar managed. "Usually."

"Precisely why your father remained behind," Freddie said. "Against his will, I might add. He would have done anything to come with us except abandon his duty."

Oscar emitted a sound very much like a snort.

"He had to command the troops if Pig Iron Kelly took it into his head to attack, with the fleet away on the royal visit. You will find your father a changed man."

With a gasp and a cry of pain, he sat up. "Davey!"

Freddie tried to push him back down. "He is well. He is in the rear of the conveyance. Oscar, what on earth is the matter? No, you must not try to climb over the bench. Oscar!"

"I must make certain. Does he still have his jacket on?"

"What on earth?" Freddie's despairing gaze found Daisy's. "He *is* delirious. A blow to the head, William—what if his brain has been damaged?"

"But does he?" Oscar persisted before William could speak. "Just tell me, Freddie. Just look. Please."

"Freddie, go," Daisy begged her. "He will not be easy until you do. He must not be so agitated—it could be dangerous."

Freddie whirled and went through to the rear. "Davey?" She slid open the door of the sleeping cupboard. "Davey, do you have your jacket on still? Oscar wishes to know. Davey?"

Daisy saw her bend, as though she were moving the bedding. Then she straightened and looked about the rear compartment, glancing over the drawers and compartments containing medicines as if to remind herself there were no hiding places. Checked the engine compartment. Bent and looked under the seats.

"Dear heaven above," Freddie said blankly, straightening to grip the back of the bench. "Where on earth is Davey?"

"He is not aboard?" Jake gripped the lever that unlatched the door. "You are certain?"

"No, he is not." Freddie clutched her skull as though she would tear out her hair. "How could we have left him behind? It is impossible! I saw him climb in mysel—"

Jake had already shrugged on the rucksack of provisions. Without another word, he pushed open the door and leaped from the conveyance into the rushing air.

12:10 p.m.

Davey Fletcher crouched behind a tumble of granite rocks on the seaward end of the airfield. The conveyance took off faster than he had ever seen it go, and that was saying something. It passed forty feet over his head, and he scrambled around the rocks to keep them between him and any anxious eyes peering out the viewing ports. Within minutes it had shrunk into the distance down the sound and his friends were safe for the present.

Now to take care of their future.

For in a blinding flash, it had become clear to Davey that the lives of Daisy and William, Freddie and the Professor and maybe even Corporal Kent had been ruined because of his big mouth. Because he had wanted to brag, to have a single moment of shining success in the eyes of a poor abused woman. It didn't matter that the woman had been lying to them the whole time—had probably lied to dozens of people as she winkled their stories and the necessary names out of them in the darkness of the gaol.

What mattered was that the loss of the ingot of Californio gold had been his fault. Therefore, he had to make it right.

The plan was simple, as all the best plans were. He had to retrieve the ingot, then hide with it until William and Daisy came back for him.

He could do that. This village looked nothing like Georgetown, but he had survived on the streets for a year after Mama's death. He could survive for the day or two it might take for the conveyance to return, and then they could pick up their lives as though this horrible experience had never happened.

He flexed his hands, which were a little banged up from the copper pot incident, but he didn't think any fingers were broken. They still wiggled and could help him eat and steal, which was all that really mattered at the moment.

At the upper end of the field, the pirates gathered around Pig Iron Kelly and Annie to admire the ingot. Kelly would allow no one to hold it, but he demonstrated its weight, hefting it up and down in his hands. Perfect. While they were all distracted—even the boys who formed the ground crew— Davey slipped into the trees and made his way unseen up the ferny, brambly fringe of the airfield. At length Kelly tired of showing off, and limped away as though Annie and the others weren't even there.

Davey had positioned himself behind the middle airship, thinking that Kelly would return to it and he could board unseen before he got there.

But they went in the opposite direction, toward a two-story white house on the street that bordered the airfield. A house larger and better kept than the others.

Well, blast and bebother it!

How was he going to get over there and inside the house in time to see where Kelly hid the ingot? He couldn't stay here now—he had to know the pirate's hiding place, and that was that. Well, nothing for it. He must sneak through the trees until they gave on to those few houses on this side of the airfield, and work his way around behind buildings and sheds. He'd figure out how to get across those two streets once he got up there.

Every man on that field knew what he looked like. But he couldn't discard his clothes and steal others to change his appearance—not his jacket, at least—because Oscar's mother's ring was still concealed behind his sleeve lining. He'd given away the secret of the ingot because he'd been stupid. He wouldn't be stupid a second time. They could tear him limb from limb and he'd never give up the ring that Oscar meant to offer to Freddie. So, since he couldn't go about openly, pretending to be ground crew, he must be invisible.

He'd had lots of practice in hiding in plain sight. It had been a while since he'd had to, but he didn't think he'd lost the knack of it.

Luckily, none of the houses seemed to be fenced off from one another. No need, he supposed. They'd stolen this village, he'd bet, so why worry about keeping each other out? He crept through an orchard, helping himself to a couple of withered apples as he went and keeping an eye on the windows in case there was movement inside. A shed provided a moment's shelter. A sand pit on the edge of the village stumped him for a moment, until he remembered that ballast bags had to be filled with something. But he made note of it as a good place to conceal himself if worse came to worst. Beyond the sand pit was a path that wound up the hill. He'd have to watch in case someone came down behind him.

Now for the first street. It was nearly deserted, except that here and there was a woman or two, and even a couple of kids, playing tag under and over the verandah of a house. He loped from one side of the street to the other, walking fast as though running an errand for his mother. Dormant gardens and bare orchards behind the houses provided cover. And just as he reached the cross street and could see the big white house on the other side, the crowd of pirates burst around the corner, talking and yelling as though they were on their way to somewhere important.

He gasped and ducked behind a rain barrel, sitting on his heels and pressing himself against the clapboard side of a shop. Through the gap, to his horror, he saw Pig Iron Kelly and Annie, going in the same direction. Had he gone to the house to hide the ingot? Or was it still in his possession?

Follow him, you big numpty, and find out.

Or follow the crowd at least. Where were they going? To a saloon, to celebrate their triumph over six innocent people?

"Coin of the realm!" someone shouted.

"With this you can buy a yacht, Kelly!" someone else called.

"How much is it worth?"

"Ten thousand pounds at least," Kelly called back. "We shall see how far we can stretch it. I for one will not be carting this to the bank in Port Townsend, with or without a yacht."

A gale of laughter puzzled Davey, who thought that in the absence of a conveyance with a secret compartment, a bank was the best place for it. But by saying *this*, it was clear he still held it. There was hope Davey could get his hands on it yet.

From behind the barrel, which was full from the storm last night, Davey watched the jubilant crowd push through the wagon doors of a big shed the size of a barn up in the next street. The sound of hammer on iron stopped at their entrance, and Davey could no longer hear.

Why would they take a gold ingot to a blacksmith?

Only one reason he could think of. They planned to melt it down. Immediately.

How was he going to get it away from Kelly now?

Hunching low, Davey took advantage of the fact that no one was looking in his direction to dash between two houses and across the street. He circled through a belt of trees and undergrowth that bordered a rushing creek, and came out just behind the forge. A huge woodpile was stacked in the yard behind it. It was also clear that this was where the coal deliveries came.

Coal. Coal came in through a chute.

Davey opened the round, ground-level door of the chute, which looked almost exactly like the one in Georgetown through which he got in and out of the Opera House. He slid down the chute and landed in a pile of coal in a mine cart. Listening carefully in case he might have been heard, he picked himself up and rolled out of the iron cart, out of sight. It was nice and warm down here in the cellar, but he could not stop to enjoy it. He did, however, mark it as a good place to spend the night.

There was enough light to see, for the huge engine that took up most of the cellar also powered the electricks. Davey could hear the wash and gurgle as water piped from the creek flowed into the boiler. Pistons pumped up and down, heaving iron scuttles full of coal on a track up through a hatch in the ceiling. Through a second hatch they came down empty, presumably after having dumped their burden at the forge.

Could he ride up to the forge in one of the buckets?

Peering up through the hatch, he observed that the track looped over a beam for support. He could leap out and watch from the beam, if—but no. He would certainly be spotted. Besides, he must hurry, and while not nearly as exciting, the wooden staircase was his most practical choice. Up he went on silent feet, then peered through the crack of the slightly open door. The apprentice assigned to shoveling coal must have abandoned his post to join the excited crowd.

From here, Davey had a fine view of the forge, from the tall, muscular smith in his leather apron and gloves with his back to him, to the anticipation on the faces of the pirates. Kelly had clearly just handed the ingot to the smith, who was turning it in his gloved hands.

"You want English guineas or Texican dollar coins?" he asked Kelly. "I have molds for both, but the guineas will go further around here."

Molds! Davey nearly fell backward down the steps. They were going to forge the Queen's face on illegal tender? How in the name of heaven was he going to stop this? For he couldn't very well load up his pockets with counterfeit coins and present them to William and Daisy, could he?

He might not have a choice. For the smith had signaled to his apprentices, who began to shovel coal and into the firebox of the forge. With a setup like this, they could build engines for steamships and airships. Melting an ingot into counterfeit coins was probably child's play. Something they could do before tea.

Despair flooded Davey's heart as he watched the smith place the ingot in a cast-iron melting pan with a shaped spout. The boiler powered a massive bellows, and the fire was ready almost before Davey could wrap his mind around the size of it. The smith slid the pan into the fire, and Annie bounced on the balls of her feet, clapping her hands in delight, her cheeks red from the heat.

Suddenly, the smith bent, as though he was craning to look into the pan. With his tongs, he hauled it out of the fire. Surely the entire ingot hadn't melted already? It had only been seconds!

The smith stared, then grabbed a wooden bucket and sloshed water into the pan.

A cloud of steam went up, and even Kelly leaned forward.

With his tongs, the smith picked up something black from the middle of the pan.

"What's this?" Kelly demanded. "Has your process discolored it? Isn't it pure?"

"I'd say not." The smith tilted the pan, and showed the assembly the contents. Davey got a flash of a very small trickle of gold and a whole lot of black cast iron. "This is all the gold there is."

"What do you mean? Speak up, Morgan, or I'll shoot you where you stand."

"It's plated," the man said, clearly unaffected by the threat. "Gold plate over pig iron and a lead core. This ain't a real ingot, sir. Someone's having a joke at your expense."

A scream of rage reverberated through the forge—a sound Davey had never heard a human being make. "I'll kill him!" Pig Iron Kelly roared. "I'll torture him for weeks, him and his motherless brat both! Death won't be too good for him!"

In sheer terror, Davey plunged back down the stairs into the cellar and hid in the dimmest, farthest corner he could find in the tangle of piping. A pandemonium of pounding feet sounded like the breaking of a storm on the floor above his head.

And then he heard something else.

A clang, as though the coal chute had closed. But instead of the familiar thunder and rattle of coal, he heard a softer sound, such as his own body had made as it landed in the shifting pile in the mine cart.

Davey shrank back into his nest of pipes.

He was no longer alone.

CHAPTER 11

OVER WHITBY ISLAND

12:20 p.m.

Ohat in the name of heaven are we to do?" Papa glanced over his shoulder, but he could not appeal to his daughters for long. Instead, he was forced to reach over and latch the door to stop its banging in the wind before it was damaged. "He is mad. He must have been killed. Our altitude was at least one hundred feet!"

"You must come about," William said. "We must attempt a rescue."

They were sailing over the channel between Whitby and the next island now, which was wild and possessed not so much as a field to set down in.

Daisy was reeling from the shock. Jake could not have meant suicide. But whether or not he had lost his head and in a moment of madness decided to go after Davey, it would come to the same thing. "No one could have survived such a fall, and into such cold water, could they?" she asked through her despair.

"We must at least look." Papa adjusted the propellers and the conveyance began to come about. And in that moment of its changing direction a couple of degrees, a cannonball screamed past them in exactly the place they had been.

Daisy and Freddie shrieked, both pitches grinding against each other in a spectral fashion that raised goosebumps.

"Steam, Frederica!" Papa shouted. "Now!"

She vanished into the engine compartment and shoveled coal as though her life depended on it. Papa piloted the conveyance at top speed on a southwest heading, putting the entire width of the uninhabited island between them and the unseen cannoneer on the headland at the mouth of the sound.

Another channel. Then a large island, dotted with farms and houses—and the ghostly grey forms of two more airships.

Daisy gasped, half rising from the bench. "Shall I help Freddie? What if they pursue?"

"They are moored," Papa said. "And we are high enough to be out of range."

"Thank heavens for Tobin's improvements to the engine," William said weakly. "We must get to Victoria with all speed."

"Victoria?" Daisy yelped. "We cannot go to Victoria."

"Yes, what about Davey?" Freddie repeated, as though she could not yet apprehend Jake's fall, nor the near miss by the cannonball, and must grasp for a fact to hold on to. "How could we have lifted and he not be aboard?"

"I saw him climb in myself," Papa objected, as though this ought to produce Davey, disheveled and smiling, from some cubbyhole Freddie had overlooked.

But Daisy knew the conveyance as well as Freddie did. She had overlooked nothing. Davey was missing, and Jake might be dead, and they were the only ones left who could do something about it.

"He obviously climbed out again," William said with a groan. "But to what end? What could he have been thinking? Unlike your friend Jake, it is not like Davey to disobey orders."

"It is not like him to give away our secrets to strangers, either," came a muffled voice from the rear bench, "and yet it happened."

"Davey told the pirates of the ingot?" Daisy's stomach sank as she realized what had driven the boy to abandon ship. He had gone to retrieve what he believed to be the real ingot.

"We were deceived, and very cleverly, too," William said. "Pig Iron Kelly had his wife already in the gaol, posing as a prisoner. Davey should not have revealed our secret. No one disputes that. But if she had been who she said she was, the damage would not have been so great."

"Well, be that as it may—Papa, why have you not come about?" Daisy demanded. "We have not an instant to lose—we must go back. Davey may still be at the airfield, and Jake—"

"Are you mad, Daisy?" Freddie demanded. "We were nearly killed just now. We must get Oscar to hospital *immediately!*"

Once again, Daisy felt as though she had been punched in the stomach, and by one of the people she loved most in all the world at that. "You are the one who is mad if you believe that a concussion—which will heal—is more urgent than our friends' lives! Don't you understand? Jake may not be dead, but if he is, that leaves poor Davey alone on an island with a band of cutthroat pirates!"

"I understand that perfectly well," her sister said, chipping words from the air with a tone like an ice pick. "But how mad must you be if you cannot see we are more than halfway to the barracks? Clearly our priority must be Oscar. Once he is in safe hands, we may turn our thoughts to Davey."

They were over the peninsula now, the farms and fields giving way to tidy neighborhoods, the streets becoming more and more crowded as they approached the Empress Hotel and beyond it, the harbor and the Birdcages.

"I can't believe it." Daisy flounced in her seat until she faced forward, crossing her arms and refusing to consider Freddie's logic. "He is not your ward, is that it? So he does not matter as much as a man who has not even offered for you?"

"Daisy," William begged, coming out of his stupefaction with an effort. Clearly he had never seen a man leap out of a flying vessel—or witnessed she and her sister in a quarrel. "We must not turn on each other in this moment of crisis. We are here now. We will land, get Oscar to a doctor, and then put our heads together to come up with a plan."

His fiancée glared at him, outraged. "You, too! I thought you cared for Davey!"

"I do care for him. But we are exhausted and injured and overwrought. We must think clearly, and—"

"I am not overwrought!"

"Margrethe Amelia Linden!" Papa set the vanes vertical for a short approach to the RCAP airfield. Thankfully, his hands were busy or he might have turned and swatted her like a misbehaving child.

Daisy was already regretting the fishwife screech of her own words. The untruth of them. The humiliation of them.

"William—darling—I am sorry." The tears came in a hot flood so that she could barely speak. "Freddie, Oscar, please forgive me. Papa, you are quite right—I am completely over-wrought, and terrified, and filled with horror. Here we are abusing poor Davey for his mistake, when we have made a worse one ourselves, in not checking that everyone was aboard before we lifted."

She pulled her handkerchief from her sleeve and sobbed into it, simultaneously attempting to blow her nose.

A faithful arm slid around her shoulders, and she found herself pulled around to weep into William's filthy coat front. "You're forgiven," he said softly.

"We will find them, Daisy, I promise," Freddie said. "And I am sorry, too. For what I said, and for poor Jake…" But she could not finish.

Oscar had nothing to say. He had lost consciousness.

The ground crew were obliged to carry him across the grass to the sick bay, Freddie walking anxiously beside him, while Daisy and William moored the conveyance themselves.

While Papa went to Inspector Kent's office to inform him of Oscar's condition, an orderly took William into the infirmary for examination. He was pronounced to be cut and bruised but fit, patched up, and released into Daisy's care.

"I was tempted to ask for a roll of bandage and a tin of sticking plasters," he confided to her as they climbed the stairs to the inspector's office. "They would come in very handy on the conveyance."

"We will do our best not to need them," Daisy assured him. "As long as we stay out of the way of cannonballs."

But with the mixed results the day had already produced, she was likely to be proved wrong sooner rather than later.

They found Papa in the inspector's office, pouring whiskey into a small glass. Seated behind his desk, Kent looked up as they entered. His face was grey, and wordlessly, he knocked back the proffered whiskey in a gulp.

"Thank you," he said hoarsely when he could speak. His color began to return. "Thank you all for rescuing him. How is he?"

He had thought they were coming to tell him of his son's death, Daisy realized. Her heart squeezed with compassion and gratitude that they were not.

"He is being examined by the surgeon," William offered. "He told us on the flight here that he believed himself to be concussed. They will not take any chances, I assure you."

"I must go to him." William stood aside to let him pass, but Inspector Kent stopped in the doorway. "Did Kelly injure my son?"

"He has been beaten by Kelly's men," William said gravely. Daisy noticed he did not bring his own hurts to the inspector's attention, brave man. "The blow that felled him also rendered him briefly unconscious, but Kelly did not strike it. In all, he displayed admirable restraint himself, while allowing his men to take out his disdain and hatred on Oscar."

"He will pay in full, and it will not be by proxy," Kent vowed in a dangerous tone. He wrung William's hand, making him wince. "You must go to the boarding house. Oscar's aunt will be frantic for news. She will have seen you moor."

"Yes, of course," Daisy said. "We will go at once."

"We will reconvene later to make a plan." Inspector Kent paused again, as though counting heads. "Where is the young lady? And the navigator?"

"Freddie is with Oscar, sir," Daisy said gently. She could not bring herself to speak of Jake. "She will need your strength, too."

With a nod, he departed, leaving Daisy, William, and Papa with nothing further to do but cross the street to the boarding house and give a much redacted report to Mrs Birch over tea and at least four different kinds of cake. It was clear that in times of great mental anguish, Mrs Birch found relief in the kitchen.

Papa did full justice to the cake while she hung on every word, first from William and then from Papa himself as he related his part in the transaction.

"But how very brave of you," she breathed. "Facing down Pig Iron Kelly alone!"

He shook his head, and smiled at Daisy. "I was not alone, dear lady. Jake Fletcher was with me. My younger daughter kept the engine at full steam so we could make a quick departure, and my elder daughter had her Colt trained on the pirates every moment. One false move, and she would have dropped the man in his tracks."

"Oh, my goodness." She was quite overcome. "The two of you sound like heroines straight out of the *Tales of a Medicine Man*."

"We do, rather," Daisy said with a wavering smile in William's direction. "But our news is not all triumphant. The smallest member of our party was inadvertently separated from us, and Jake plunged into the sound to go in pursuit of him. We could not even return to attempt a rescue, for we narrowly missed being hit by a cannonball. Truly, we have gained two and lost two. I am very much afraid that makes us the worst rescue party ever in the world."

"Jake," Mrs Birch repeated in astonishment. She did not, Daisy noticed, disagree. "Plunged into the sound."

"From a height of one hundred feet at least," Papa added.

"Good heavens. He will have been killed—if not from the

impact, then certainly from the cold water. What are you going to do?"

The fact that their hostess had echoed Daisy's own words only made her cross at herself. Since when had she given up hope? Until they rescued Jake and Davey—or had proof that no rescue was possible—she would choose to hope.

For had she not proven that hope could triumph against all odds? Up on the pinnacle cell in Santa Fe, where would she and Freddie and Annelise Strauss be if they had given up hope? Food for vultures, that was what. Or on the island of the pelicans in San Francisco de Assis with that massive wave barreling down upon them? Drowned, if not for hope. And action.

So there you were. She would hope, and act, and that was that.

"When Inspector Kent and Freddie join us, that is exactly what we intend to decide," Papa was saying. "May I have another slice of that lemon poppyseed cake? How clever you are to have guessed it is my favorite."

"Do not worry about Jake, Mrs Birch," Daisy said, helping her father to the cake. "He tells us he has been through a similar experience and survived. Somehow I think cold water and a few pirates are all in a day's work for Mr Jake Fletcher."

Whitby Island
1:15 p.m.

Davey hardly dared to breathe. But coal dust being what it was, his nose began to itch with the urge to sneeze. He must not move. Must not even exhale, with an intruder in the coal cellar who would waste no time hauling him up in front of

Pig Iron Kelly. Who would probably throw him in the forge himself, to be burned alive.

The urge to sneeze overwhelmed him. He held his breath and his whole body spasmed.

A tiny sound escaped his throat.

"Davey, are you here?" came the rasp of a whisper. "Is that you?"

Of course a pirate would say that. But that sound he'd made could have come from a rat, couldn't it? All was not yet lost. Davey did not move a muscle.

"Davey? It's me. Jake."

Who was Jake? He didn't know anybody called Jake. That was a pirate's name if ever he'd heard one.

"I was with Professor Linden when we handed over the ransom."

Which didn't answer his question, but now Davey vaguely recollected a tall young man who had been at the professor's elbow as he'd bolted past, his whole being intent upon reaching the protection of Daisy's Colt and begging forgiveness before a bullet tore through his back.

"Come on, Davey," the voice said, somehow conveying a smile in his whisper. He was moving now, making a circuit of the walls as Davey himself had done. "Don't make me regret my plunge out of the conveyance into the sea."

He must have moved in his surprise, for the soft steps turned and came closer.

"I lost my head a bit when they said you weren't aboard. We were only a hundred or so feet up when I decided to hop out and come find you."

"You jumped out of a moving vessel?" Davey squeaked. It

had been moving fast, too. As fast as he'd ever seen it go. "To find me?"

"Aye. Soaking wet, I am, and a nice seaweed scent about me. Glad it's nice and warm down here. I thought sea-bathing in Scotland might have prepared me for the water here. But I was wrong."

All right, a pirate would never say something like *that*. But still, the parts and pieces didn't add up. "*How* did you find me?" He'd thought he'd been so clever, dodging and hiding. If this person had found him so easily, how many others would be able to as well?

"Always watch your back. I came ashore under a cannon emplacement just west of a gravel pit. The cannoneer would have seen me jump, so there was nothing for it."

"For what?" Davey asked, puzzled.

Jake had paused at his hiding place. "All right if I join you?"

"Aye. I'm behind the water pipes. Watch your head."

In a moment, a man folded himself on to the floor beside him. His sleeve, wool and very wet, brushed the back of Davey's hand. He did smell a bit seaweedy, but it wasn't unpleasant.

"You wouldn't know it by my uniform," he said, removing his jacket, wringing it out, and draping it over a warm pipe, "but I've always been a dab hand at the dirty work." Jake made his confession with what Davey thought was admirable modesty. "Once the job up there was done and the gun spiked, I removed his two six-shooters. You may have one if you know how to use it."

"I do," he said cautiously. "Daisy taught me. But please, I still don't know who you are or how you found me."

A Colt revolver was pressed into his hands. His lessons

with Daisy in his mind, he checked the hammer and saw that all six cylinders were loaded. The weapon's owner had not even had time to draw.

"I saw you at the sand pit on my way down. Followed you. And when all that ruckus broke loose upstairs, I took my opportunity and slipped into the coal chute, just like you did. What caused all the fuss?"

"Pig Iron Kelly ordered the smith to melt down the ingot for counterfeit gold guineas. Turns out it was a fake we've been so careful to carry all the way from the Royal Kingdom."

Jake's body shook in a silent gale of laughter. "Oh, how I wish I'd seen it," he said when he could speak. "It was Professor Linden's idea. A bit of pig iron for Pig Iron. The real one is safe as houses, back in Victoria."

Wait—they had *made* a fake ingot? Just since yesterday? "I wish someone had told me," Davey said reproachfully. "I thought it was the real one, and since it was my fault it got handed over, I thought it was up to me to get it back." He was silent a moment. "Daisy isn't very upset, is she?"

"I've never seen a woman more distraught," Jake said. At Davey's indrawn breath, he added, "I'm a bit sorry there wasn't time to explain to her what I meant to do."

"You jumped out of the conveyance." Davey shook his head. If not for the soaked clothes, he would never have believed it.

"Aye. She'll think I'm dead, and when she knows I'm not, she'll likely chew the skin off my face with the lecture to end all lectures."

"She will," Davey agreed. "My dad used to say that when Mum was mad at him. About the skin on his face."

Jake chuckled. "Mine, too."

Davey squirmed into a more comfortable position. "So that's one question answered. What about the other? About who you are, exactly? And how you came to be on the conveyance before you jumped out of it."

"It's a bit of a long story, but the short version is that Miss Freddie is a school friend of my intended, Maggie Polgarth."

"Oh!" Davey sat up. "I've heard her talk about Maggie. And her cousin, Lizzie, who is engaged to an engineer aboard Lord Dunsmuir's vessel. And someone called the Lady. She admires Maggie very much."

"Does she, now? I like her even better, then. As it happens, we flew them to Denver from New York on *Swan*, but I wasn't able to get acquainted much while I was on duty."

"Jake! You're Jake Fletcher, the Hollys' navigator?"

"I am indeed. And what's more, we'd flown the professor out of the Royal Kingdom of Spain and the Californias after the Rose Rebellion, and put him on land in Reno. He went to Santa Fe and—"

"—and that's where we started looking for him," Davey said. "After we solved the bride's murder in Georgetown."

"That's what Daisy said, too, when I bumped into them on the harbor in Victoria. It was like a homecoming for four. I was pleased that after all their adventures, they had finally found their father."

"And we would all be in Victoria right now, eating roast beef and Yorkshire pudding, if it hadn't been for me and my stupidity." Davey hung his head, though he hoped Jake couldn't see his eyes getting wet.

"It wasn't stupidity, lad, to want to make things right," Jake said gruffly. "How were you to know? It wasn't as if we could explain, there on the field with a dozen rifles aimed at us. It was vital to the plan that Kelly believe the ingot was real."

That was true. Davey began to feel marginally better. Except— "Now our friends will think you're dead."

"The Lady you spoke of and my adopted family have thought that before, and I proved them wrong," Jake said. "In fact, I've had a wee bit of experience along these very lines. We have our work cut out for us, lad. We're going to make these pirates wish they'd never been born."

"We are?" Davey wasn't sure whether to be intrigued or terrified.

"Oh, aye," Jake said with satisfaction. "We have to do *something* to amuse ourselves until we're rescued off this rock."

CHAPTER 12

VICTORIA

2:00 p.m.

After consultation with the doctor, Inspector Kent decided that his son would recover best where there were people at hand to wake him up at intervals and test his responses. People whom he trusted. People who were not housed in a building that would be the air pirates' first target should they choose this moment to attack the defenseless city.

So two burly constables carried him across the field on a stretcher, from which he spent the brief journey protesting to Freddie that he was perfectly capable of walking. In Jake's unexpected absence, Mrs Birch had changed the sheets and made his bedroom ready for an invalid, with a comfortable armchair pulled up next to the bed and the filmy drapes drawn so as to admit a gentle light.

"Quite the nicest room in the house," he mumbled to his aunt. "So tired."

"Then you must allow yourself to sleep," she said in a

soothing tone. "Freddie will keep watch until it is time for one of us to wake you and take her place."

"Inconvenience," he managed as his eyes slid closed.

"Not at all," she said. "We have years of lost visits to make up for."

As the door closed softly behind her, Clementine's misty form passed through it and hovered anxiously at the foot of the bed.

Oscar had fallen asleep in moments, in the way Freddie understood military men often did, when sleep must be snatched from the jaws of duty.

"It is all right," Freddie told her in a whisper. "He has been examined by the doctor, who says that outside of the headache, which should pass, he needs rest and peace in which to heal. The inspector thought it best to bring him here. It would not be suitable for Mrs Birch, my sister, and I to keep vigil in the men's barracks."

Clementine came to the other side of the bed and sat upon it. The mattress did not indent, but when she laid her hand upon Oscar's forehead, it seemed to Freddie that some of the lines of strain in his face smoothed out just a little.

"There, you see?" she said. "He is better already with you here."

Clementine's hand slid to his shoulder, then down his arm, as though checking for injuries.

"Are you able to communicate?" Freddie asked her. Sometimes the dead could speak, but the sense of their words varied greatly, from riddles that made sense only to them, to the ravings of insanity, to sheer waves of incoherent emotion.

Clementine's lips moved, but there was no sound.

"I see. Well, I am no lip reader, sadly. We will just have to make do, won't we?"

Clementine nodded. Then she made a gesture that Freddie had little trouble interpreting. *How can you see me?*

"I told the inspector I am a medium, but that is not entirely true. I have been able to see those who have left this temporal sphere since I was a child."

Such a burden to lay upon a child.

"The burden lies heaviest upon my father and sister," Freddie said with regret. "Their biggest fear is that someone will find out, and have me committed to an insane asylum."

Clementine's eyes widened with horror. Then her gaze dropped to her son, and she glanced up, one eyebrow raised.

"No. He does not know."

The other eyebrow rose, over a meaningful glance. Freddie fidgeted with the glass of water on the night table, straightening it just so.

"I do not know if I will tell him," she said reluctantly. "If … he indeed proposes. We—goodness, it is uncomfortable saying these things to his mother. We have only known each other three months."

With a fond smile that conveyed a delightful memory, Clementine gazed in the direction of the barracks, as though she could see through walls and air to where her husband and his sergeants plotted the defense of Victoria without the aid of airships.

"Your courtship was brief but powerful, too?"

Clementine nodded.

"Are you tied to this house, or to Inspector Kent particularly?"

To Marcus. And Oscar.

"And your brother and his wife because you loved them, and possibly visited them here?"

Another nod.

Oscar sighed and moved restlessly, and Freddie leaned nearer, laying a soft hand on his forehead, smoothing the coverlet. When she looked up, Clementine had gone. She rather wished she hadn't. It was refreshing to be honest about herself with someone outside her immediate family. Oscar's mother was good company.

For a ghost.

2:45 p.m.

Daisy did her best to reason with William, to convince him that he ought to be in bed like Corporal Kent.

"I suffer nowhere near the injuries that Oscar does, and I am needed in the inspector's office with your father." He touched her cheek as they stood on the verandah in the long rays of the January afternoon. The scent of wet grass and baking bread drifted in the air. "I promise I will mix up an unguent for my cuts and bruises, and a soothing lavender concoction to simmer in Oscar's room, after dinner. But for now, we are needed, and there isn't a moment to lose."

"Then I am going with you." She took his arm with a firmness that was not to be argued with.

"I would expect nothing less."

There was nothing quite as forlorn as an empty airfield, possessing only the deserted conveyance. Nothing quite as visible from the air, either. As they crossed the grass, Daisy shook off the persistent sense of an impending storm.

They found Papa, the inspector, and two sergeants

standing before a chart pinned to the wall of Kent's office. Blue pins marked the locations of villages, it seemed, while red ones indicated pirate airships.

Three red pins were clustered at the head of the inlet that divided Whitby Island.

"There should be two more here," Papa was saying, pointing to a bay on an island to the north. "San Juan. We saw them as we passed over, but they did not lift in pursuit, thank heaven."

One of the sergeants said, "So that's five pirate vessels accounted for as of this afternoon. We've had word that the two that had been on Saturna had divided, leaving one there and the other gone to the island with the salt springs, there at the south end."

Inspector Kent looked grim as he moved the red pins into position. "They are moving closer, into attack formation. See how the ships form an arc." His finger described it.

"Have you ground cannon?" Papa asked. "Companies of rifles?"

"Yes and yes," Kent said. "But they are volunteers at the gun emplacements. I hesitate to call them up until our plans are definite. What of the other ships remaining in Kelly's fleet?"

"We have no information more recent than Monday," the second sergeant said. "Our final patrol before the contingent departed for Edmonton was fired upon. At that time, there was one on Camano and four on Horcasitas Island."

Inspector Kent sighed. "So they know our detachment at Port Townsend is short of vessels, too. Blast these royals and their insufferable need for a show."

"I'm quite sure Pig Iron Kelly knows how many forks are

in the barracks kitchen, and whether there are eggs in a given RCAP vessel's pantry, sir," the sergeant said with an air of gloom. "He knows when to choose his moment, that's certain."

Daisy had crossed to the window, which overlooked the airfield. A glint in the sky caught her eye, and she sucked in a breath. Her heart began to pound. Talk of attacks and gun emplacements suddenly became more than mere advance planning.

"Daisy?" William said. "What is the matter?"

She peered through the glass. "Something is coming," she said.

Whitby Island
3:00 p.m.

Standing in the communications cage, Davey had his jacket off, trying to get the ring to come down the sleeve. He had already written his note to Daisy, having borrowed a bit of paper and a pencil from the box where most crews kept them. All he had to do was get the blasted ring out and send them both to Victoria.

He almost … had … it …

And then he felt a vibration in his feet, and the stern of Pig Iron Kelly's third vessel dipped.

"Jake!" he whispered. "Someone's come aboard!"

"Never mind the ring, it's fine where it is." Jake closed the door of the pigeon's message compartment and sent it on its way after the others. "Get your jacket on. We have to hide."

Davey might have been able to fit through the hatch of the communications cage, and the eight-foot drop wouldn't be so bad, but Jake would never be able to escape that way. No sooner had this unfortunate conclusion crossed his mind than he heard the familiar call. "Up ship!"

He and Jake gaped at each other in horror.

They had not left anything behind in the cellar of the smithy to raise suspicion, but Davey had been looking forward to a meal and a warm place to sleep before they moved on to the next stage of the plan. Now what were they going to do?

Jake cast about, but the cage held nothing but pigeon racks and a chest of equipment, no doubt to make repairs. And now the deck pressed up against Davey's feet and they were under way. The sound of booted feet thudded in the corridor.

"This way." Jake climbed up the empty racks, right to the ceiling. "Come on!"

Victoria
3:10 p.m.

Every man in Inspector Kent's office abandoned the map and joined Daisy at the large mullioned window. "What is it?" the sergeant asked, squinting into the light.

And suddenly Daisy knew. "They are pigeons," she said in astonishment. "A flock of them, coming in to—goodness, where are they heading?"

"The holed ship," Papa said suddenly. "Only one still possesses a communications cage. This is too far out of the ordinary not to mean something. We must go down and meet them at once."

The damaged ships had been floated to a hangar on the far side of the field, which owed its situation behind a copse of tall trees, Daisy felt certain, to an order not to spoil the view of the government officials in the Birdcages. As Daisy and William and the four others spilled out the side door, they could see the last of the brass pigeons, wings humming bravely, dive for the open door of the hangar and vanish inside. By the time they crossed the field and jogged down the path through the trees, an aeronaut mechanic was waiting for them outside, waving a turnscrew.

"You've got to see this, sir," he called to Inspector Kent. "I've never seen the like."

There were nearly two dozen pigeons hovering at the gate to the communications cage of Number Seven, bumping gently against the grille.

"Let them in, man," Inspector Kent shouted. "All of them."

They boarded Number Seven and headed aft at a brisk trot. When they arrived, the pigeons had slotted themselves into every single available rack, and those that could not had set down upon the deck. Inspector Kent gave swift directions, dividing the devices up among them all to see what news they carried.

Every compartment was empty.

"What on earth …?" Papa murmured to himself, closing the door of the last one in his assigned rack. "Be sure to reset their addresses to neutral so they will not return. Not until we discover what this means."

Daisy reached into the remaining one of her assigned pigeons and felt a piece of paper. "I have something!"

She unfolded it and made a sound very much like a squeak, then clapped her free hand to her mouth. She must not give way to emotion now. Not with five men staring at her. She read it aloud, her voice shaking.

Dear Daisy and William,

I hope you reached Victoria safe. I am well, and so is Jake. We are going to reek havock until you come. When we have done as much damage as we can, we will go to No. 13 to be rescued. Here are lots of pigeons. Now Pig Iron Kelly can't talk to his other ships. It was my idea.

Yours sincerely,

David Fletcher

PS: Tell Oscar it's still safe.

"JAKE IS ALIVE," William said in wondering tones. "You were right, Daisy."

"We must have faith in each other, I see, even when it makes no sense," Papa said when Daisy could not speak past the lump of tearful gratitude in her throat.

"Tell Oscar *what* is still safe?" Inspector Kent asked. He held out his hand for the note. When Daisy gave it to him, he read the scrawled lines rapidly, but they did not provide further enlightenment.

William cleared his throat. "Oscar had in his possession a diamond ring, which I believe belonged to his mother."

Daisy resisted the urge to reach out a comforting hand as grief suffused the inspector's face. He tapped the note with the back of one hand and fought for control. "What in heaven's name possessed him to take my wife's engagement ring on this voyage?" he said in hoarse confusion. "She left it to him in her will, for his bride. But … I thought he had left it with his aunt for safekeeping."

She must find her voice. She must speak up for the poor young man beside whom Freddie sat vigil. Who had been through hell for her sake.

"I believe he meant to propose marriage to my sister during the crossing from Port Townsend to Victoria," she said. "But Papa insisted that she and I travel with him, so Oscar never got the chance."

"When we were set upon by the pirates on the shore," William said, "Davey's jacket sleeve was torn. In the scuffle, none of them saw Oscar slip the ring to me. I put it down Davey's sleeve between the lining and the wool. Davey wishes us to know it is still there, as yet undiscovered."

"Clever Oscar," Daisy said. "And clever Davey, to have sent us all the pigeons." She thought of the map with its three red pins as she considered the racks of shiny devices. "From all three ships, it appears. Quite a feat to have pulled off undiscovered."

"Let us hope they *were* undiscovered," Papa agreed. "Now Kelly is isolated. Either another of his ships must happen to report in, or he must lift and go elsewhere to commandeer a few with which to communicate."

"In that case," one of the sergeants said, indicating that they should follow him and disembark from the disabled Number Seven, "now would be a very good time to attempt a rescue. You will be in far less danger today than tomorrow, if they have not yet discovered their loss."

"It is still daylight," Daisy said by way of agreement. Surely there was enough time.

"Not for long." As they emerged from the hangar, William glanced up at the skies, which were once again piling up with clouds to the west. "They will not have had time to reach the wreck of Number Thirteen. It took us hours to make only half the trek up the inlet before we were discovered. We must stick to their plan. We certainly cannot sail into Kelly's airfield and collect our friends as though they were waiting for a steambus."

"Davey said they meant to wreak havoc," Papa put in. "The pigeons were only the beginning. Their mission is not yet over if they freed the devices less than an hour ago."

"I wish the boy had thought to send the ring with his note," Inspector Kent grumbled. They emerged from the belt of trees and he gazed at the boarding house on the far side of the airfield. "It would set my son's mind at rest."

"Perhaps they thought the pigeons would be intercepted by pirates," William said. Daisy, her hand snug in the crook of his elbow, felt him controlling the urge to bristle at the implied criticism of their ward. "Or perhaps they were interrupted in their task, and could not complete it."

"We won't know until we ask them," Daisy said, before exhaustion and strain got the better of both men. "So we will make the attempt tomorrow?"

Inspector Kent nodded at his sergeants, who returned to their duties in the barracks. He paused at the foot of the steps that led to the entrance hall of headquarters. "If we can assume Kelly will not fly at night to go fetch a supply of pigeons, then perhaps that is safest. A sensible saboteur would do his worst at night in any case, with time left over to reach the rendezvous point by dawn."

"Best case," William said cautiously.

"It's Davey," Daisy pointed out. He was safe. And Jake was alive and with him.

They had every reason to hope.

Whitby Island
3:15 p.m.

DAVEY HAD ABOUT ten seconds before someone came in to send a pigeon and found out they were all gone. He swarmed up the racks—which, luckily, were bolted to the wall—and found Jake balancing on the open top of the wall.

"Into the fuselage," Jake ordered, and boosted himself up on to the catwalk.

Davey followed with the alacrity of a spooked cat, grabbing Jake's hand to be pulled up the rest of the way. He reached the catwalk just as the door opened directly under their feet.

A man's foreshortened head was just visible below. "Council of war," he said to someone behind him. "Pig Iron's like to have an apoplexy. It's all hands on deck for us poor squabs."

"I ent never seen someone get the better of Pig Iron Kelly," his companion said in an awed undertone, as though the walls had ears and might tell on him. "I'd never have believed—"

"Where are all the pigeons?" The first man scratched his head under the leather strap of his goggles. "I could've swore we had a few."

"Nobody wants to talk to us."

"That ent news. Too late to borrow a couple."

"No matter. Someone else will signal Saturna."

"You're right. Flight's so short we could beat the thing there. Did I tell you about the time we—" The door closed with a clang and the voices faded back down the corridor.

"That was close," Jake said over the whistling of the air

between fuselage and gas bags, and the beating of the treated canvas over the struts.

They gained altitude and began to come about.

"Sounds like they mean to attack Victoria for true," Davey said.

Jake shook his head. "Not now, anyroad. They're heading north, but—" The catwalk fell out from beneath their boots just a little. "They're descending already."

That meant they were going to an island close by. Not that it made a whisker of difference. Just when he'd thought they had a perfect plan, it had all gone awry. "I wish I hadn't been fussing about the stupid ring," Davey groaned.

"Wouldn't have mattered," Jake told him, ruffling his already windblown hair. "We barely got the pigeons away before we lifted. Couldn't do much about ourselves. Besides, this could be a good thing."

"How?" Davey demanded plaintively. "We don't know where we're going. But even if we did, now we've got no pigeons to tell William and Daisy we've changed islands."

"We do know where we're going. To an island with an airfield northwest of Whitby. I've seen it on the charts—San Juan." He pronounced it the Californio way.

Davey began to recover his spirits. "And we know what we're going to. A council of war."

Jake grinned a feral grin that told Davey he was enjoying this far too much. "What better place for a couple of saboteurs?"

CHAPTER 13

SAN JUAN ISLAND

3:45 p.m.

*D*avey was thankful for his warm wool jacket, shabby as it had become, for they could hardly leave the safety of the catwalk until they knew all the crew had disembarked. His stomach, which had seen nothing since the apples he'd picked hours ago, growled so loudly that Jake could hear it.

"If that happens again, we'll have to hope they think it's the rigging." Jake, having prowled from stern to bow on the catwalk to get the lie of the ship, now sat with his forearms on his knees, his fingers loosely linked, listening to the ground crew moor the airship.

"Sorry," Davey said. "I was in gaol this morning, don't forget. All I've had to eat today is a handful of cold porridge and two wrinkly apples. And yesterday, raw oysters. I had to close my eyes to eat them."

Jake made a face in sympathy. The ship bobbed, telling them that the airship's crew had disembarked. They heard shouts and whistles from the airfield, but up in the fuselage as they were, could see nothing but the canvas surrounding them.

"We'll sit tight awhile," Jake said. "Then we'll have a wee bite from the provisions in my rucksack. If they survived their sea-bathe."

Cheered by this prospect, Davey settled next to Jake, cross-legged.

"The layout of this boat is familiar," Jake mused. "I wonder if it was a Royal Aeronautic Corps ship in its previous life."

"Maybe," Davey agreed. "Bet it was stolen."

"You'd win that bet. But at least I know where things are. Such as the arms locker."

"Are we going to break into it?" That would make noise, but all the same, it sounded exciting.

"We'll need to decide on that," Jake allowed. "Food first."

"When did you eat last?" Davey wanted to know.

"Breakfast at the boarding house. Your friends are all staying there with me. A lady named Mrs Birch runs it—turns out she's your Oscar's auntie."

It sounded so homey and friendly, to have friends who would invite you to stay with them. "Is she one of the society of absent friends?"

"If that's the boarding-house ladies, then aye, she must be. She took to Daisy and Freddie like they were long-lost sisters. Like she already knew them."

"Do you have any family?" Davey wasn't certain Jake would like him asking questions. A man as handy with weapons as he might want to keep his life a secret.

"I have a brother called Snouts. And then the Lady, and my

Maggie. The others who grew up in the Lady's house are like brothers and sisters to me."

"Snouts isn't really his name," Davey protested, trying not to laugh. "Does he have a big nose?"

"It used to be bigger. He's grown into it," Jake said with an answering smile. "He's actually my half brother. Stephen McTavish. He'd rather I used that name, but my father was Fletcher, so I figure I'm more entitled to that than anything."

"Fletcher?" Davey repeated.

"Aye. It's a bit confusing. My mother was with McTavish when she had Snouts, then left him and married Gil Fletcher. A couple of years later I came along, and then she died. Fletcher was a steamship man, so we were left with an aunt in Glasgow. One thing led to another, and we wound up in London, where we met Lady Claire Trevelyan—Malvern, now. We stole her landau and she tracked us down and bombed us."

"Bombed you!" What sort of people did Freddie call friends, over there in London?

"It all turned out well. We threw our lot in with her and it's been quite the life ever since."

But never mind about the Lady, whom he would probably never meet. There was something far more important Davey wanted to know. "So your name is Fletcher, too? And your dad is Gilbert?"

"Yes, for all the good it does me. Don't know where he is. Never heard from him again. He's probably dead."

It couldn't be the same man. It was completely impossible. Yet how many Gilbert Fletchers could there be who were also steamship men?

"He is dead," Davey said, taking a chance. "He died in an

accident in the railway yard in Denver, working on a steam locomotive, because there isn't much call for steamship men in the Fifteen Colonies."

Jake stared at him.

"He died when I was little, but I remember he had dark hair, like mine, and a big laugh."

"And … and your mother? Where is she?"

"She died over a year ago. In Georgetown, where we were living. Consumption, I think. Her name was Charlotte."

"Are you saying that …?" Jake seemed bewildered.

"I'm saying that my father was a steamship man, too. His name was Gilbert David Fletcher, but Mama always called him Gil."

"We have the same father?" Jake appeared to have been poleaxed.

Davey was nearly completely convinced, and if he hadn't been, that odd little saying about chewing the skin off somebody's face would have clinched it.

"I don't know for sure, but it seems so." Jake didn't look thrilled about it. Maybe he and his brother with the big nose had been family for so long there wasn't room for anybody else. Maybe Davey should have kept his big mouth shut and pretended he hadn't noticed the name at all.

"I can't believe it," Jake finally managed. "Snouts and me … we have another brother!"

"Is … is that all right?" Davey asked cautiously.

"All right?" Words seemed to fail him. Then he threw both arms around Davey and hugged the breath right out of him. "It's more than all right. I never dreamed of such a thing. A brother! All the way out here, on the edge of the continent, I find a brother! And kidnapped by pirates, to boot. That makes you part of the family like nothing else can."

Davey had never had a brother—the closest he'd come to a sibling was Lin, and she had gone to the river canyons with her cousin, the woman who had declined to be a princess. After he'd lost Mama, he'd resigned himself to being alone and scrabbling a life for himself on the streets until he was old enough to work in the silver mines and make his fortune.

And then he'd met William and Daisy and Freddie, and everything had changed.

And now everything had changed again, and he wasn't at all sure how he felt about it.

"What's the matter, Davey?" Jake held him at arms' length. "I'm not much of a prospect as far as brothers go, but our Alice will vouch for me when she and Ian get back."

Davey almost laughed. "It's not that. It's just that … I haven't had any family in a long time, except for William and Daisy. And I don't know how to be anybody's brother."

"Well, I can't say I'm very good at it, either," Jake admitted. "But if you like, we can be friends first. And then being brothers might come more naturally to us. What do you think?"

Davey wanted to talk to William and Daisy. They would know what to do. But in their absence, his life might depend on Jake. And having a good friend, someone he trusted, in this present situation sounded like a very, very good idea.

"Friends," he said, offering his hand.

Jake took it solemnly. "Friends." A single shake. Then, "I think it will be safe to go down to the galley now, where it's warmer, to see how our victuals survived." He grinned. "I think the occasion calls for a celebration anyway, don't you?"

Davey did, rather. Although he supposed the victuals wouldn't include cake.

Sadly, the cake had not survived its sea-bathe, as they discovered a few minutes later when they unwrapped it. But they did find everything else in the rucksack in order—the pork pasties in their waterproof tin tasted like heaven, and the fresh water in the canteen was cold and sweet. Jake pulled the knife from the sheath inside his still damp boot to cut up the dried apples. It was a perfect feast.

And speaking of knives …

"They took Oscar's things off him—he had an equipment belt, and one of Mr Bowie's knives, like yours," he said to Jake as they ate. "Can we have a quick look after?"

"Don't see why not," Jake said. "It'll have to be quick, mind. We want to get off this ship and find a place to hide for the night."

"Why not aboard?"

Jake shook his head. "Just our luck they'd launch again, and if we were asleep, we'd wake and not know where we were, unless it happened to be back on Whitby."

Good point. Jake was a navigator, after all. Davey imagined that knowing where he was at all times would be important to such a man.

"We should just steal this ship and fly ourselves to Victoria," Davey said.

"It's a possibility," Jake allowed. "One of several."

"What are the others?"

"Well, you told our friends we were going to wreak havoc. What did you have in mind?"

Davey had given that a lot of thought while he was

sneaking about trying not to be killed. "How many cannon emplacements do they have, I wonder?"

"Pig Iron Kelly has one on the rising land on either side of the airfield on Whitby. I did for the one, as I told you, but the other is still in action. Wouldn't surprise me if he had a similar pair here."

"We could put sand in the barrel and the breach," Davey said. "Spike them, too."

"Good, depending on how much time we have. What else?"

"Wet their clothes and put sand in them."

"Annoying, but not what I'd call havoc," Jake said. "Also very noticeable. We want things they won't notice until it's time to use them, preferably under fire."

Davey didn't notice clothes until it was time to use them, but never mind. "We can set the airships adrift."

"Oh, they'd notice that for certain." He grinned. "But that's where I would start, too. A ship they can't use is one less to attack our friends with, innit?"

Which gave Davey another idea. "What if we *don't* set them adrift—what if we steal one and tie the others to it, and tow the whole lot to Victoria?"

"Do we know how many ships are moored here?" Jake sounded thoughtful, as if this were actually a practical plan, not an eager flight of fancy.

"No," Davey said, feeling encouraged nonetheless. The galley had no viewing ports, and they'd best not show their faces anyhow.

"When we go out, we'll have a look. What else?"

"That's three ideas. Your turn."

Jake cleaned the knife on his pant leg with deliberate care, and slid it back into his boot. "You probably wouldn't like my ideas. So we'll consider them a last resort."

Davey swallowed. "Let's go see if Oscar's things are aboard."

It wasn't likely. The knife probably decorated the belt of a pirate now, the equipment belt too. So Davey was more resigned than disappointed when they could find no trace of them. But the arms cabinet was more encouraging.

Jake made quick work of the lock with a strange little tool he kept in his pocket, and surveyed their find with some satisfaction. A row of rifles and shotguns stood at attention in the upper section, and in the drawers below were stored at least a dozen revolvers. Sacks of bullets occupied the bottom drawer, and half a dozen bombs of the kind he had seen on the island of the pelicans in San Francisco de Assis lay beside them.

He hadn't expected that.

He bent closer. Sure enough, there was the Royal Kingdom's cross and crown stamped into the iron. By what criminal act had they come to be here?

"How are we going to carry all this away?" Davey straightened up. The weight of the Colt he already carried was enough for him. He eyed the little bombs, though, like the old friends they were.

"We're not." Jake broke a shotgun and checked the chamber. "This isn't loaded. They must be awfully sure of themselves. We could take their ammunition and toss it down the nearest rabbit burrow."

The poor rabbits. Davey didn't like that at all. "Wouldn't it just be easier to make off with the ships?"

Jake gave it a few seconds' consideration, and nodded. "It would be nice to deliver them to the RCAP with armories intact, all right." He moved to close the cabinet, but Davey darted in and snatched two of the bombs. They fit in his palms like they were meant to be there. Jake shook his head at him, but said only, "Come on. Let's see if we have enough daylight to do for those gun emplacements."

They crept the length of the ship, cautiously checking each doorway in case someone still remained. But in the case of this vessel, at least, all hands had been required at the council of war. They reached the gangway in the stern and with a final reconnoiter, disembarked as quickly as they could, then used the bulks of the ships as cover to dart into the woods on the fringes of the airfield.

"I counted five," Davey panted as he caught up to Jake.

"I wonder how many are in the fleet?"

"And if they'll come here tonight so we can set them *all* adrift."

But Jake shook his head. "They won't take a chance on an RCAP ship returning and finding the whole fleet in one place. Odds are they'll divide it."

"And send pigeons to tell the others what they plan. Best I take care of those while you do for the guns, Jake." And the gunners. He gulped.

"Aye. Divide and conquer. Meet there." He pointed. "See that fir? Its branches form a shelter at the bottom, both soft and dry. I'll look for you under it. Take the rucksack in case I'm longer than I expect."

Jake melted into the trees and Davey couldn't help but be grateful he had a good reason not to go with him. The sun slanted through the treetops in a way that told him he had about an hour of daylight left. The airfield was deserted, with only the boys in the ground crew left to keep watch, and they were fifty yards away at a firepit, pushing and shoving each other and laughing over something.

Davey tossed the rucksack under the tree, then boarded the first of the two ships that must have been here when they arrived, since they still had their pigeons. Snatching up the pencil and a bit of paper in the communications cage, he scribbled a message.

On San Juan. Kelly called a council of war. Reeking proper havock.
Watch for ships.
    D. Fletcher

This vessel only had three pigeons, but even if others came back after calling the council of war, that was still three down. He set them on their way with a sense of satisfaction.

Now for the other. He wouldn't risk the gangway again—too visible.

So he slid out the pigeons' chute and plummeted to the grass.

"Oy!" a voice said. "You scared her!"

Davey froze, still on his hands and knees.

A girl about his own age marched over to him, her pinafore stained and ragged, her reddish braids coming undone. She was so skinny it hurt to look at her. "Thanks a lot."

"Scared who?" he croaked. Was she alone? Had any of the boys in the ground crew heard?

"My chicken," the girl said in disgust. "I've been trying to catch her for an hour, and won't Kitch be furious if I don't come back with her." A guilty look crossed her face. "I forgot to latch the gate behind the house."

"Sorry," he said. Sure enough, there was a black hen under the floating gondola of the last ship, about twenty feet away. She was eating grass and investigating the possibility of worms.

He had to get rid of this girl, and release the next batch of pigeons.

"Who are you?" she said. "After nearly landing on her, you'd better help me catch her."

"I'm crew," he told her.

"Crew isn't a name. We're all crew. I'm Jenny. Did you come over from Whitby?"

At least he didn't have to lie to her. "Yes. I'm Davey. I've got some bits in my pocket. Let's see if we can tempt your hen out from under. Then I've got to return to duty."

"You sound like my dad. He was an aeronaut."

"Was?" He broke off bits of pasty crust, tossing them so they formed a trail. The hen looked up with interest. Crust was better than worms, to a chicken's mind. In Davey's experience, at least.

"Yes." She sounded sad. "Pig Iron Kelly killed him. He was RCAP. They brought us here and now I belong to Kitch. He's a cook on this ship you just came out of, but we live in the village."

The hen took the first bit of bait.

"Wait. You said *us*. Who was us?"

"My mother. She died." Her mouth trembled, but she controlled it, as though tears were no longer allowed.

"Is he good to you? This Kitch?" The hen walked to the next bit and ate it.

She shrugged. "I don't think he likes me—he wants to hit

me. I saw him hit my mother and she never woke up. He thinks I'm going to tell Kelly, but I never would."

"Why not? The man killed your mother. He deserves some kind of punishment."

"Kelly'd kill me just for complaining," she said. "Look. It's working."

The hen had made her way nearly to them. "Go around behind her," Davey said. "I'll offer her this last bit, and when I do and she's distracted by it, kneel down and grab her by the leg."

"The leg." Jenny looked at him as though he'd lost his mind.

"She won't see your hand. Birds see things coming from above, not from under."

Jenny did exactly as he said, and in less than half a minute, had the struggling hen in her arms. She beamed at him. "Thanks."

"What are you going to do with her?"

She looked down at the bird, then shifted her in the way he'd seen May Lin hold Perdida, the little white hen she'd found in the tunnels under San Francisco de Assis, with one hand under her feet and the other arm around her to make a nest. The hen settled, as though she'd been held this way before. As though she were more of a pet than dinner.

"Kitch told me when they landed he's going to butcher her tonight. There's some kind of shindig happening after the council of war."

"Butcher her! Why didn't you let her go and pretend she was lost?" A shindig meant liquor, he would bet. And drunken pirates would be less likely to notice missing ships—or be able to stop them if they did notice.

"He'd probably serve me up in her place if I didn't come back with her." Something about the hopelessness in the girl's green eyes, her thin cheeks, her shoulders hunched under the ragged clothes as though they expected a blow, made Davey's heart clutch with compassion. Time was when he had been exactly like this girl. No, he'd been luckier. There had been no Kitch for him.

"Don't you want to get away?" he asked. "If you could?"

"Of course I do. But how can I?" She looked about the airfield. "We're on an island. And they're everywhere in these islands, Kelly's men. You know that."

Trapped, and no one to help, no door to slip through to escape. Except one. Davey made up his mind. "I'll help you. Come with me."

"Where? You're just crew." The hen made a sound when her arms tightened. "You're not going to tell Kitch what I said?"

"I'm crew, all right. But not on any air pirate's ship," Davey wasn't sure what Jake would say about it, but at least he wouldn't serve the girl up for dinner. "No one needs to go back to Kitch, ever, and be afraid of being butchered for the rest of their life. Not you. And not that hen."

CHAPTER 14

VICTORIA

5:15 p.m.

Sunset was thickening into twilight when Inspector Kent once again presented himself at the door of the boarding house, to be ushered inside by his sister-in-law. Daisy and Freddie heard the two voices in the hall and came to the head of the stairs, but since the father wished to see the son, they were already mounting the steps. In Oscar's room, the invalid pushed himself further up on his pillows. Freddie wondered if he thought he ought to salute.

Clementine came through the wall, one hand touching her mouth as though to contain her emotion at seeing her two men together again, and at peace.

Inspector Kent sat upon the edge of his bed. "At ease, my boy. We'll have no formalities here." He gripped his son's hand as though he had feared someone might have done away with him since he'd been brought here after their return earlier in the day. Then he looked up at Freddie and the others. "We've had another pigeon. Actually, seven pigeons."

159

"Davey is at it again." Daisy's smile was infectious, and Freddie couldn't help smiling, too.

"He is. When he returns, I am very tempted to write the Walsingham Office and recommend they give him a job." The inspector handed William a crumpled note, which he read swiftly and handed to Daisy. It went in rapid succession from Freddie to her father to Mrs Birch to Oscar.

"What is our plan?" Oscar said.

He sounded stronger, though that was likely Freddie's imagination. There was still the night to get through, with its task of waking him every four hours. Clementine stood next to her husband, her misty hand passing through his shoulder in a caress.

"This new information must change our thinking," the inspector said, with a glance as though he had felt something. "If Pig Iron Kelly has called a council of war, he will lift at dawn. I must call up the volunteers and make sure what few defenses the city has are ready to meet him." He looked pained. "And I must inform Lieutenant-Governor Dunsmuir."

Daisy and Freddie looked at one another. They had learned in Port Townsend that this was James, Lord John Dunsmuir's younger brother, who had been elevated to the knighthood upon his appointment by the Queen.

"Will that be painful, sir?" Freddie ventured.

Inspector Kent shook his head. "In a manner of speaking. He is not as experienced in government as his predecessor. To add to that, he is distracted by personal matters. His redoubtable mother, the Dowager Countess, seems to have fallen in with a woman called Isobel Churchill and is involving herself in politics in Charlottetown. An engagement of some years has just been broken off, and every eligible female in the territory seems to want to comfort him in his loss." He sighed. "As sympathetic as I am for the man and his difficulties, it is more of a job than it should be to get anything done around here."

"But an imminent attack by air pirates is different than the affairs of government," William said. "Surely he must respond to that."

The inspector adjusted his goggles and rose from his son's bed. "Let us hope so. Professor Linden, I wonder if you might accompany me? Your knowledge of the matter would be a great help."

Papa looked gratified, and nodded. "I shall be honored. Then, if you will allow me, I might accompany you to rouse the volunteers."

"Thank you, but my sergeants will take care of that as soon as I have Dunsmuir's permission to give the order. It is Dunsmuir I need help with—if nothing else, to help me keep my patience. I shall collect you in the landau in twenty minutes, if that suits?"

The inspector departed with a last word of encouragement for Oscar, whose face wore a wondering look at this change in his father. Freddie had told him of what had happened upon his return, but he still could not quite believe it. It was a case of actions speaking more loudly than words. And the inspector, she had observed, was a man of action.

"Twenty minutes," Papa said. "That presents a problem. While I have serviceable clothes now, thanks to my daughters, I have no evening rig. Kent may trust in his uniform, but I cannot very well meet the governor of the territory dressed so informally, in traveling gear."

Mrs Birch eyed him up and down. "My dear late husband

was not so large a man as you, Professor, but I wonder if I might scare up a few things for you to try on."

"Evening clothes," Daisy groaned. "We should have thought of that while we were in Port Townsend."

"A town that does not lend itself to such," Freddie reminded her.

Clementine's movements caught her attention. She was pointing urgently up at the ceiling, and pantomiming pulling on trousers and a coat.

"Mrs Birch," Freddie said, "I wonder if there might not be something in the attic that might fit? Belonging to a family member, perhaps?"

Their hostess looked astounded. "My goodness, you are a young lady of astonishing perspicacity. I had completely forgotten about my father-in-law's trunk. He was a man of substance, like your own dear papa, and about the right height, too." She looked anxiously at Papa. "You will not mind if they are slightly out of fashion?"

"I do not regard fashion in the least, dear lady," he said. "Allow me to come with you, so as to save time."

"Dear me, yes. Twenty minutes!" she said as they hurried out, Clementine gliding in their wake. "Only Marcus would say such a thing. And he is *such* a stickler for promptness, too."

"We *are* about to be attacked by air pirates," William said as their voices faded away upstairs and the four of them were abruptly left alone. "That would necessitate some haste."

Freddie could not help but laugh. "She is a dear lady," she said. "Fancy our father going to meet the Lieutenant-Governor."

"I am glad we are not required to do so," Daisy said. "Clever Davey, to give us this new information. The inspector may concentrate on the defense of the city, but I should prefer to fetch Davey and Jake off that island."

"It is the closest one to Victoria," Oscar said. "Kelly has made it convenient for us, at least."

"I would suggest a rescue by night, if he had only specified a meeting place as he did in his first message," Freddie said. "Are we to assume that if he is releasing pigeons from airships, that he and Jake will stay in the vicinity of the field?"

"I do not believe we can safely assume anything," William said. "It is the quickest way to a fatal error. But we know one thing. He and Jake have already concluded they must set the ships adrift. *Watch for ships*, he wrote."

"If I were with them, I should certainly do so," Daisy agreed. "That would be the very definition of *reeking havock*, would it not?"

"I wonder…" Oscar seemed to be examining a vista through the window that they could not see.

Freddie leaned forward in the chair she had commandeered as her own at his bedside. "Yes? What are you thinking?"

"I think that we must not hesitate to reconnoiter the island," he said at last, coming back to them in an instant. "Your conveyance can be of no use in the defense of the city, but it certainly can be useful to spy out the situation."

"It must be tonight," Daisy said, "if your father is certain they will attack at dawn."

"Davey knows this, too," William said, nodding. "But I disagree with him on one point. We must not merely watch for ships. We ought to intercept them."

"All right," Daisy said. "Let us do exactly that." Again that smile flashed that Freddie was coming to love. Daisy smiled much more often these days than she ever had back in England. "For then the RCAP can commandeer them to mount a counterattack."

"Exactly," Oscar said with satisfaction. "When shall we go?"

"We?" Freddie frowned at him. "You are not setting foot outside this room."

"I am perfectly well." Oscar's brows knit. Under other circumstances it might have been intimidating, but not from a man in a nightshirt, propped up by pillows. "I am quite capable of flying."

"Yes, but the conveyance is not capable of carrying all of us, and Jake and Davey, too," William replied before Freddie could speak.

Which was just as well. Freddie would not have been nearly so practical in her remarks.

"We must take the minimum number to get the job done," William went on. "Daisy to act as navigator, myself as pilot, and Freddie as engineer."

"Papa will not like that," Daisy warned him. "Not at all."

"Neither will Father," Oscar put in. "He will take it as disobedience of an order."

"But he has given no orders," Freddie said. "Not to us. Only to Papa."

"That's true." A twinkle of mischief came into Oscar's eyes that dissolved every trace of intimidation. "And I cannot imagine that their errand to Cary Castle will be concluded until well into the evening. It is, if I am not mistaken, the cocktail hour, and good form must be observed, even in a crisis."

Footsteps sounded out on the landing, and Clementine glided into the room, looking pleased. So it was no surprise to

Freddie when her father came in for his daughters' inspection looking every bit the gentleman, rather than a vagrant in a deceased airman's Prussian blue coat.

"Papa!" she said with no little admiration. "Don't you look handsome."

And he did, with black trousers and a gray swallowtail coat, a white shirt gone only a tiny bit yellow with age—it would never be noticed in a room lit with electricks—and a silk cravat of peacock blue and green that should have been shocking, but on a man of his size was merely elegant. Mrs Birch had even located a pearl stickpin for the cravat, and boots that had been hurriedly buffed to a shine.

"Well done, Mrs Birch," Daisy said. "Your own father must have looked equally as dashing."

"He did, at that, though of course the professor is a hale man in the prime of life." She blushed. "I am only happy we could find something in time, for I just heard the landau outside."

The words were hardly out of her mouth when a peremptory knock came at the door. Papa and the inspector puttered off, and when Mrs Birch came back upstairs to Oscar's room, her blush and agitation had faded. She glanced from one to the next. "You look as though you have news. Has something happened while I was seeing your fathers off? How could that be?"

In the end it fell to Oscar to tell her.

Poor Mrs Birch went to her room with a glass of wine and a cold cloth for her forehead. Clementine remained, but only Freddie saw her shaking her head, half admiring and half horrified at what they meant to do. And with perhaps the smallest hint of regret that she herself could not go with them.

San Juan Island
6:20 p.m.

As darkness fell, the ground crew—not one of which was older than twelve—abandoned their posts and ran away across the field. As in the village on Whitby, there was one house larger than the others, lit up and filled with men who had come for the council of war, and it was in the direction of this that they ran. Davey wondered if there was someone in the kitchen to feed them, or if they were merely looking for the food and entertainment that the shindig was sure to provide.

"They don't maintain a watch?" he asked Jenny as he peered through the pine branches of their hiding place.

She wriggled, as though needles had gone down the back of her neck. The hen was roosted up on a branch next to their heads, tucked close to the trunk and unaware of how close she had come to being stew.

"Why should they?" Jenny replied. "None of the townsfolk would dare touch these ships. Enough people's fathers and mothers have been shot already. Blast these needles. Whose idea was this, anyway?"

"Mine," came a voice out of the dark, and before Davey could even react, Jake had rolled under the branches of their concealment and sat up. He was panting, as though he'd run quite a distance. "I can hear you from ten feet away."

"Sorry," Davey whispered. "We thought the place was deserted."

"It is, but not for long. Who is your company?"

Davey bit back a dozen questions about what he'd done to the gun emplacements and what had taken him so long to get back. "This is Jenny. She lives with Kitch, the cook from the first ship we sent the pigeons from. Jenny, this is Jake Fletcher." A warm feeling tumbled through him, a mix of companionship and admiration and the possibility of actual family. "My brother."

"I am pleased to make your acquaintance, sir," Jenny said, shaping the words as though she had not said them in a long time. "And up here is my hen, Sootie."

"Your ... hen?" Jake's voice sounded blank.

"Yes, she's roosted up on this branch just above us. You can't really see her in the dark. She is a black hen."

Davey heard a sound he had never expected to hear on this hell's-half-acre of an island. Laughter, muffled in a coat sleeve, but laughter nonetheless.

"Welcome to the flock," Jake said when he could speak. "I assume you're coming with us? You and, er, Sootie?"

"If you'll have me, sir."

"Oh, aye, if there are chickens involved, we'll have you. In my circle of friends, it's a sign of good character. Tells us a person is to be trusted."

"I am, sir. Trustworthy, I mean."

"Never mind the sir, Jenny. We're all friends here. I'm just Jake." Davey felt something pressed into his hand. "We may as well finish these pasties before we take our next steps."

"The guns?" Davey asked.

"Done for," Jake said. "The hill to the north had one of Mr Gatling's nastier inventions. Very complicated bit of machinery to be foxed by something so simple."

"Sand?"

"Yes."

"And the gunner?"

"Quite a surprise it will be, to find the gun unmanned. I predict that in the heat of the moment, the replacement won't think to check the cartridges. Just start firing. And then there will be a merry show." Jake munched his pasty in happy anticipation. "Would the bird like a bite of supper?"

"I'm sure she would, sir—Jake," Jenny corrected herself. "She's awake."

An eagle dispatching a salmon couldn't have made more of an excited fuss than Sootie over her prize. "She was hungry," Jenny said apologetically, her mouth full. "So was I."

"Now she'll want the rest of it. She's as bad as Mrs Morse aboard our ship," Jake complained. "So, Davey, have you let our Jenny in on the plan?"

"Not without you." To Jenny, he said, "We're going to tie these five ships together and steal them."

She gasped. "You never are! They'll kill you!"

"They'll have to catch us first," Jake said dryly. "If they do, you're to say that we forced you at gunpoint."

"You have guns?"

"Oh, aye," Davey said. "Colt six-shooters. And—" A hand closed on his shoulder and he stopped. He was doing it again. He must learn not to give away their secrets, even to a new member of the flock. Whatever that meant. "But they won't catch us."

"Once we tie each ship's bow line to the next ship's stern line, we'll release all the mooring lines. Jenny, can you work vanes?"

"Yes. All of us can."

By *us* Davey gathered she meant the ground crew, all children. They started young, these pirates. Trained to be crew and inducted into the life so young that crime seemed a perfectly normal way to make a living. If you valued your hide.

"Good. You'll go in ship number three, in the middle."

"But that's Pig Iron Kelly's own flagship." Her whisper caught on the jagged edge of her fear.

"No help for it. It's the way they're moored. I'll go in the first one, there, closest to the village. The one with the most risk. Davey, you'll bring up the rear in number five. I'll depend on you both to read the wind and keep an eye on my direction to guide your ships. All right?"

"But who will be your engineer?" Davey asked. "Oughtn't I to act as pilot while you tend the engines?"

"I won't even ignite them until we're high enough to be out of firing range," Jake said. "Then, we'll head west, as silently and swiftly as we can. We can't go at speed in case our lead ropes break, so we don't want them to detect a single whisper of our passing."

"All right," Davey said.

"Not a sign," Jenny whispered, clearly overcome by the danger and yet forcing herself to bear up.

"We'll loose the ropes in order. Stern lines tied to bow lines. I'll do that," Jake said. "Then loose the gunwale lines, then last, the second stern line on three and five just before you board. Clear?"

"Clear," they said together.

They had only one chance. There was no room for error. Silence and stealth were paramount.

Davey slid his hands into his jacket pockets and touched the reassuring weight of the Viceroy's bombs.

∿

Silent as shadows, Jake and Davey slipped between the pirate airships, knotting bow and stern lines together. Davey didn't know much about knots, but he did know a gunner's knot when he saw one. William had taught him how to make them in case the conveyance had to be moored during a storm. It would only draw tighter and tighter with the exertion of these ships. As Jake worked the knots, Davey stayed low to the ground and loosed the gunwale lines, first on number three, where Jenny, with Sootie firmly under one arm, had safely boarded and brought up the gangway, and then on two and four. On five, Jake shook his hand in a silent *good luck* before Davey ran up the gangway, brought it up, and then headed to the gondola to work the vanes.

There wasn't much light, but the vane controls were easy to find, right next to the navigator's table. Without the engines ignited, nothing else would work anyway. Through the viewing port, he could see the clouds being pushed away by the freshening wind.

That wasn't good. The airships would have vanished into the cloud cover with no one the wiser. Now the light from the rising half moon would glint off their clumsy caravan, turning the grey fuselages white and drawing the attention of every pirate who happened to be outdoors.

But no. He couldn't think like that. They would lift, and in no time at all they'd be out of firing range. Safe.

His vessel pressed up under his boots. Jake had released the last mooring line.

Four followed, and then three. Moonlight glinted on the aft vane of number three as it straightened—Jenny knew her onions. He straightened his own so that the ship would not veer to one side and snap its lead line. A moment later, Davey was looking down the slope of fuselages, like giant elongated bubbles rising off the bottom of a glass. And then number one dipped as Jake boarded, his gangway went up, and the whole string of them fell up into the sky.

Davey laughed with delight, then clapped his free hand over his mouth.

Stealth and silence.

Up ... up ... the airfield fell away, he could clearly see the lights of the houses glimmering in the dark ...

And then the wind caught them.

Davey gripped the vane controls with both hands, compensating for the push of the wind, which insisted that they go north instead of southwest. The caravan of ships was supposed to be rising, but instead, it was buffeted sideways, out of formation. No, he couldn't allow that to happen—if a line snapped, the precious ships would be set adrift and wind up in the Tsar's icy kingdom. Oscar and the RCAP needed these ships!

He leaned on the vane levers, feeling the resistance as the unpowered ship wanted to acquiesce to the wind. Jake had to start the engines of number one *now*. He had to. Otherwise they weren't going to get to Victoria. The pirates would shoot them down and he'd never see William and Daisy and Freddie again ...

But they were still too low above the village. The pirates would hear.

Jake, for pity's sake, start the engines!

What had happened to Jake? Had he taken a fall? Davey hadn't actually seen him board—the fuselages had blocked his view. What if he'd been set upon and dragged away and there was no one at the controls of number one at all?

Davey's stomach clenched and the pork pasty threatened to come back up.

He had to do something. The pirates would see them any second now, being blown sideways instead of floating straight up as they would have on a calm night. Even a rifle could bring them down if enough of them were fired all at once—and he had no doubt there were enough arms in that village to do a proper job.

Davey made up his mind.

He abandoned his post and ran to the rear of the gondola. No point igniting number five's engine—he couldn't fly backward, and to try to push the others ahead would be like chasing so many chickens, all wanting to go their own way.

No, he must take care of the problem at its source.

When he let down the gangway, the wind nearly knocked him off his feet, to say nothing of freezing his face.

Security line, you idiot!

He clipped it to his belt and walked out on the gangway, gripping its ropes for as long as he could. Below, he could see they were still floating over the village—farther—farther—

The roof of the largest house slid into view, fifty feet below.

Farther—

Davey pulled the Viceroy's bombs from his pockets.

He yanked out the firing pins with his teeth.

More roof. More. There!

Standing on the lip of the gangway, his security line run out to its very end, he let the bombs fall from his fingers.

They clanged like an alarm bell as they disappeared down the chimney of the pirate headquarters.

CHAPTER 15

CARY CASTLE, VICTORIA

7:00 p.m.

Lieutenant-Governor James Dunsmuir resided in lonely splendor in Cary Castle, situated impressively on a rising sweep of ground crowned by granite outcroppings and spreading Garry oaks. It was a few minutes' walk from the family home, Craigdarroch Castle.

"He doesn't live at Craigdarroch, never has," Inspector Kent murmured to Professor Linden as they waited to be announced. "That is the earl's home when he and Lady Dunsmuir are in town."

In Rudolph Linden's mind, Cary Castle was not a bad substitute in which to house a younger brother. There was the requisite crenellated tower of baronial stone, but for the most part it was simply a large and elegant house with an imposing prospect. As they were shown into the reception room, he could see the lights of Victoria spread out below, terminating at the sea several miles away. The reception room boasted three enormous arched windows, and when Linden looked to the leftmost, in the first glow of the rising moon, the snow-covered peak of Mount Baker formed a ghostly backdrop for the low-lying bulk of San Juan Island.

The pirate stronghold was literally within sight of Her Majesty's government, and yet he was entertaining guests instead of rousing the country to its own defense?

The air was filled with chatter and the music of a string quartet at the far end of the room. Under twinkling chandeliers, the guests moved about in evening dress, laughing over drinks as though nothing more than the weather were under discussion. Several young ladies clustered near one window, glancing at the Lieutenant-Governor as though daring each other to approach him.

The butler escorted them over to Sir James, who was a weedy man of around thirty who did not exactly look up to his job. Linden was thankful to Mrs Birch's father for the loan of his clothes, for even he, with all his experience of gaols, cut a more imposing figure than this man.

"Sir James, Inspector Marcus Kent and Professor Rudolph Linden to see you," the butler said, and wafted away to marshal his footmen to service.

Linden and the inspector bowed.

"Kent, good to see you," Dunsmuir said, looking puzzled. "Did my secretary put you on the invitation list? You're not a donor to our fledgling opera company, are you?"

An opera company in Victoria? Linden wondered if Mrs Birch appreciated opera.

"Indeed not," Inspector Kent said. "I am here on a matter of urgency. I need your help."

Dunsmuir looked exhausted. "You and everyone else in this room. We are supposed to be talking about opera, and instead every man Jack has been put up by his wife and/or daughters to ask for an introduction to the Duke and Duchess of Cornwall when they arrive the day after tomorrow."

Linden felt a prickle of alarm. Surely the royal visit must be postponed!

Inspector Kent ground his teeth. "I have no interest in introductions. The royal couple cannot come. We are almost certainly going to be attacked by Pig Iron Kelly and his air pirates in the morning."

"At dawn," Linden put in.

Dunsmuir looked him up and down, his gaze catching on Linden's borrowed cravat. "Professor … Linden, is it?"

"Yes."

"Do you know Simon Bodey, the dean of the university? Over there, standing in front of the second window with my —with my former fiancée, Miss Annabelle Yates, the young lady in white, and her parents."

"We have corresponded, but have not met in person," Linden said. "Sir, you must listen to the inspector. It is urgent."

"Yes, yes, all in good time. Come, let me introduce you."

Inspector Kent made a noise in his throat that could have been a growl or an assent, Linden wasn't certain. But there was nothing for it. He would rather have called upon the dean at a time and place of his own choosing, to introduce himself and discover whether the post for which he had left Edinburgh in another life were still waiting for him. But as with much that had happened over the last two years, his own choice often went a-begging.

Perhaps he ought to take control now, when he was in such august company, and force this odd young man to listen to them. At the moment, it seemed they were simply being used an an excuse to join the group containing the woman who had thrown him over.

"Dean Bodey, Doctor and Mrs Yates, Miss Yates," he said. "You know Inspector Kent, of course. Allow me to introduce Professor Linden."

"Rudolph Linden," he said, shaking the dean's hand and bowing to the others.

"Good heavens," the dean said, his pince-nez dropping off his nose in his surprise and swinging on its ribbon. "Not the Rudolph Linden formerly of the University of Edinburgh?"

"Yes, sir. Allow me to offer my apologies for my late appearance."

"Late! I should say you're late. By two years, sir!"

There was nothing he could say to refute that. It was quite true.

"Was he supposed to have been here sooner?" Miss Yates asked with a charming smile. Her blonde hair was piled on her head in the new fashion, her gown cut low but still modest, her corset creating a waist of willowy slenderness. Pearls glimmered in her ears and at her throat. She was a perfect fashion plate, but Linden would put either of his daughters up against her and lay bets as to who would come out ahead in intelligence, bravery, and kindness.

"I was to take up a post, but I was delayed," he said.

"By what?" Bodey was clearly determined to get his answer now.

"A combination of things," Linden said mildly, "the most significant of which was amnesia due to a blow to the head, along with some months in a Californio gaol, just before the

Rose Rebellion secured the Viceroy's throne and the usurper was killed."

"Gaol!" Mrs Yates exclaimed.

"Amnesia?" her husband echoed, looking interested.

"Yes. I was involuntarily conscripted into the old viceroy's engineering corps and forced to do brute labor until I was rescued."

The Yates family gaped at him. Dunsmuir wrested the young lady's attention back to himself with an effort. "There's a reason to miss an appointment if ever I heard one," he said jovially. "I hope you kept the position open, Dean."

"Indeed I did not," the man said, staring at Linden as though the only word he, too, had heard was *gaol*. "Blenkinsop has the post. He was my second choice."

Linden had never really believed that the position as head of the Faculty of Engineering would have been held for a man who had vanished as thoroughly and unwillingly as he. But some part of him had hoped. The part that had remembered the name *Bodey* after a head injury when he could not even remember his own family, and had wound up in the Wild West town of Bodie hoping to find his way. The part that now laid to rest any belief that he would be making the university in Victoria his academic home for the remainder of his career.

But it still hurt. Just a little. Laying dreams to rest always did.

"If I might have your attention, Sir James," Inspector Kent ground out, "the pirate attack requires that I call up the volunteers at once. May I have your permission to do so? *At once.*"

Dunsmuir turned reluctantly to the man fuming on his left. "Yes, you said something about that. Dash it all, man, are you sure this is necessary right now? We are expecting

Adelina Patti at any moment for dinner and a private performance."

At any other time, Linden would have been seized with excitement at the prospect of being in the same room—the same town, even—as the world-famous diva. But not when this very house might be reduced to rubble by breakfast time tomorrow. For what easier target could there be if not the Lieutenant-Governor's mansion here on its grand hill?

Linden pointed at San Juan Island, now only a dark mass in the strait. He opened his mouth to speak, and—

—an explosion so large that they could see the flames from here lit up the sky. A moment later, the windows rattled.

Miss Yates shrieked and fell back against Sir James.

Her mother crumpled to the floor in a faint, forcing Dr Yates to catch her.

Linden could not imagine what was happening. All he knew was that Daisy's young ward and a brave young navigator were out there—and he devoutly hoped it was they who were wreaking havoc, not the pirates experimenting with munitions for tomorrow.

Dunsmuir set Miss Yates unceremoniously aside and clutched Inspector Kent's uniform by the buttons. "At once, man! Call out the volunteers at once! We are under attack!"

"Yes, sir." Kent saluted smartly. Linden had to admire his self-control. Then he grabbed Linden's sleeve and hustled him out of the room, where every thought of opera had vanished and all the ladies and half the gentlemen were shrieking and running about in a state of panic.

"That will be our friends' work," Linden said as he leaped into the landau.

The inspector ignited it and in moments they were rolling down the hill.

"I certainly hope so," Inspector Kent agreed.

"I cannot imagine what they've done, but I hope they are still in one piece."

"As do I. For our part, we are going straight to Macaulay Point, where we have guns emplaced. I will send emergency tubes to the volunteer corps commanders and my own men from there."

"And then?"

"All our men know what to do," the inspector said grimly. "I have drilled them relentlessly enough. But just to be sure, I will order them to fire on anything in the sky larger than a pelican."

"What about the royal visit?"

"One thing at a time, Professor. If we succeed, the Duke and Duchess may come as they like, and welcome to them. If we fail to stop this attack, well ..." He cleared his throat. "Let us hope it does not come to that."

San Juan Island
7:25 p.m.

Davey had barely got the gangway up and secure than the force of the explosion pushed poor little number five with such violence that its fuselage bumped number four, which crashed into number three, which ... oh dear. At least, he imagined that was what would happen. He didn't know, for he was flat on his face on the teak deck, dazed from the impact. Wondering what he'd done.

Get up and look, you gumpy.

He made it to his feet, thankful that his arms and legs still worked, and unclipped himself from his line. He staggered forward along the fuselage deck and down to the gondola, whose viewing port gave him a fine look at what had happened below.

The island was in darkness, except for the village surrounding the big house. The houses that remained were lit in shades of red and amber as those closest to the big house burned like massive signal fires. Of the big house, there was nothing left save a glowing hole in the ground that must have been the cellar.

Davey grimaced at the destruction his impulse had caused. Similar bombs had not had nearly such an impact when he'd thrown them before. He'd hoped merely that it would slow the pirates down a little and distract them while their airships stole quietly away overhead. What kind of bombs had those been?

"If you weren't the pirates, I'm very sorry about your houses." He was rather glad Freddie wasn't here in case the ghosts of everyone down there came after them, all screaming at him for what he had done.

And finally, there came the sound he had been waiting for. Jake ignited the engines in number one, and in a couple of minutes Davey was once again yanked off his feet as number five's ropes tightened with a snap and the ship abruptly began to make way.

Security line. Security line. Where is it?

Davey was not very good about remembering such things, but if he didn't learn his lesson once and for all, the next jolt was likely to break his neck. He found it at last and clipped it to his belt, which made him feel slightly better.

Vanes! He'd forgotten his duty!

He covered the gondola's deck in one bound and grabbed the levers. It wasn't until number five moved reluctantly into line behind number four that he was able to breathe properly again. Number three, he noticed with a shake of his head, was following number two as meekly as a lamb, in perfect position. Jenny had probably clipped her safety line on well in advance, and tied one around Sootie to boot.

Then again, Jenny hadn't blown up a pirate's lair, had she? Or even thought to put a bomb in her pocket.

Davey began to feel better.

Now the moon glinted off the open water. The island was behind them, and Victoria ahead. What a triumph! Davey inhaled a great breath of relief. For thanks to Jake's work earlier, not a single shot or cannonball had whistled through the silent night.

Just a few more miles ...

The wind was freshening, and the lines grew more taut, though Jake was not pushing their speed at all. Better to travel slowly and keep everyone together than to increase the steam and risk breaking a line. Davey had all he could do once more to keep the vanes from submitting to the wind and turning to one side. He leaned on the levers, watching the bow's position. He must keep number five right behind number three, not four. Four and two might blow about a bit, but if he and Jenny could keep in line behind Jake, they would be all right.

A great wave of joy surged through him as they made the shores of the great island—he had to resist the urge to dance a jig as he leaned on the levers. In just a few minutes they would land. A few minutes after that, he would see William and Daisy. He would find out if Oscar was all right. And he would make sure Freddie was out of sight, take off his jacket, and slide the ring out for Oscar. He would be so happy that—

Ping!

"What was that?" Davey demanded of his little ship.

Pyanggg!

Were those *bullets?* Striking the gondola? Davey was ashamed to hear the sound that came out of his mouth. They were practically safe as houses and now someone was *shooting* at them?

And not a single pigeon aboard to send and tell them to stop!

Number five juked violently to the left and Davey's feet flew off the deck. If it hadn't been for the security line, he would have been thrown against the viewing port. As it was, he swung in the air just long enough to gape through the aperture.

Just long enough to realize the line tethering him to number four had been severed.

And he was falling up into the starry sky with no control whatsoever.

7:35 p.m.

By order of the Commander
Macaulay Watch Station
Cease fire at once.
Friendlies incoming per RCAP. Repeat, friendlies.
Cease fire!

Daisy screeched as another bullet clanged off the undercarriage of the conveyance. The first had pinged off the iron step of the retractable swing. The second frightened them all half to death. The next would pierce the conveyance's iron hull, and then—

"Take us up!" she cried to William.

They had barely been in the air ten minutes when every

plan they'd made had gone off the rails. First the wind had come up and blown away the clouds they had been depending on for cover. Then the terrible explosion had sent her heart into her throat with fear for Davey and Jake. And now this?

"Why are they shooting at us?" Freddie cried from the engine compartment, where she hung on to the lever that increased the steam as though her entire body weight might get more power out of the engine.

"I think we're in the way," William said grimly, his hands busy on wheel and levers.

"The way of what?" Daisy searched the darkness below. Would she see the flash of muzzle fire from this height? By the time she saw it, would it be too late?

"That."

Something in William's tone made her whirl to face forward, and she gasped.

For coming through the sky straight at them was a sight not one of them had ever seen before—nor would they ever again. A caravan of ships. Four of them, tied together fore and aft, floating as fast as one ship's engines could tow them toward safety.

"It's Jake!" Daisy cried. "Jake and Davey, bringing us the ships!"

"Oh, well done." Freddie leaned on the rear bench, panting. "Well done indeed!"

"We thought we might be their rescuers, but it appears we are to be their escort," William said, half laughing. "I do not know whether to be proud or disappointed."

They drew even with the lead vessel and could clearly see Jake at the helm. He grinned broadly and waved, then held up a hand in triumph.

Five fingers.

He pointed behind him at the caravan, then shook his fists over his head as a prizefighter might at winning the match.

"Wait—William—"

"I will come about. There are only four. Did he mean his own plus four? Why five?"

In half a minute, Daisy and Jake faced one another across a chasm of air, dark forests lying hundreds of feet below. Thank heavens the shooting had stopped. It must have been a mistake. Someone had finally told the volunteers that any ships coming in by night were not manned by pirates. At least, she could only hope so.

Jake was watching them, still smiling.

Daisy held up a hand. Four fingers, her thumb well tucked in.

The smile fell from his face, and he leaned away from the helm toward the viewing port as though to look back at his prizes.

"William, look out, he's going into a turn. Why is he doing that? We will collide!"

William set the vanes vertical and the conveyance evaded disaster just long enough, presumably, for Jake to count the trailing ships. When he straightened his caravan, Daisy could see him beckoning frantically for them to approach.

"Closer, William," Daisy reported. "Something is wrong."

Now she could see his face again through the viewing port. His mouth moved in exaggerated speech.

Davey. Davey on ship— He spread his fingers to indicate *five.*

"Oh, dear heaven," Daisy said in horror.

7:40 p.m.

Great snakes, what was he going to do?

Davey did his best to control his fear as the caravan of grey pirate ships fell away below him, leaving poor number five at the whim of winds and maybe even—if things went badly—waves. To the best of his knowledge, the gondola had not been holed. He had no idea if the fuselage had been, but even if it had, he would likely still have two of the three gasbags still in operation. He was not falling, in any case. Quite the opposite. But he needed to gain control somehow, or he would be tossed ever higher until he reached the point where the cold would cause the lifting gas to contract. Once that happened, the ship would plummet to earth, and any re-expansion of the gas would be too slow. It would *not* be a slow glide to a soft landing.

He pushed the vane controls over to horizontal, and with his foot, pulled on the second set so that the ship would go into a slow turn. He must keep her going in circles, that was it. Use her urge to rise in his own favor.

For it was certain that he could not run back and ignite the engines. For one, he did not know how, though given enough time, he might be able to figure it out. He could operate the conveyance's engine, after all, so how much different could it be? But in the time he took to do it, the ship would have been lifted up into the cold, and then no amount of steam to the engines would bring the vessel out of free fall.

No, he must keep her here, going in circles, taking her back down little by little with the vanes, until Jake landed at the airfield. He would see at once that he was missing a ship, and would come to his aid.

All Davey could do was hope that if there were pirates on the other islands, as Jake thought, they wouldn't have seen the explosion. Hadn't got word of the ships being commandeered. Wouldn't be up here patrolling or attacking somebody, and see number five sailing in lazy circles for no reason at all except that she was adrift. Or stolen. In which case, they would board her. Or fire their mounted guns. Or—

No sooner had he pictured several dreadful scenes than the moonlight pouring through the viewing port was abruptly blotted out.

Davey cried out in fear.

7:45 p.m.

"There!" Daisy said, pointing. "There he is!"

The ship was smaller than the ones Jake had been towing, but it was still a full sized airship with its own mounted guns. It was describing a wobbly circle in the night sky, clearly visible under the moon, with the backdrop of the great island's farms and forests below it.

"Clever boy," William said with satisfaction. "He has no engine, so he is using the vanes and the wind to keep himself from drifting until help comes. I would have done exactly the same."

"Take us closer," Daisy said. "He must know we are here before another moment passes, poor darling."

They ascended to bring the more nimble and maneuverable conveyance abreast of the airship's gondola. Daisy had been so afraid that he would have been blown out to sea, or worse, shot down by mistake. To see him bravely sailing in circles nearly brought her to tears.

She waved both arms, the shadow of the conveyance racing along the gondola, and Davey's head swung abruptly toward her.

Stark terror melted into astonishment, and then to her own dismay, he started to cry.

She caught her breath in a sob.

"Come on, you two," William muttered. "This is no time for tears."

"I know," she choked. "But he knows we are here. We are both weeping with relief."

"The question is, how are we going to get him to the airfield?" Freddie said, leaning once again on the back of the bench so that she could see. "Can one of us board in order to ignite the engine?"

"Impossible," William said. "Our two fuselages will bounce off each other, forcing the gondolas out of reach."

Daisy's mind raced through any number of options, most of which were completely unworkable. Unbidden, a memory flashed into her mind. *What's the matter with you lot?* Davey had demanded in a similar situation. *Why don't you use the swing?*

Then, as now, their friend Tobin's improvements to the conveyance might just save a life.

"The swing," she said urgently. "I will capture Davey's bow line and fasten it to the rear of the conveyance. Our only solution is to tow him to the airfield as Jake was doing—and quickly, before the wind comes up any higher."

"Take a security line," Freddie said, moving aside so Daisy could pass her. "I will operate the swing."

"Never fear," Daisy said. "I have learned that lesson thoroughly."

She clipped it to the gun harness she still wore, while William brought them forward to the grey airship's bow. With the conveyance in position, Freddie allowed some of their pent-up steam to escape, enabling them to match, then slow the other ship's wind speed to their own cruising speed.

At the rear door, Daisy called, "Ready, William."

He set the vanes vertical and the conveyance dropped slowly down in front of and slightly below the bow ring of the pirate airship to which the rope was knotted. Daisy opened the rear door and her hair blew straight back from her face under the force of the wind. She would not have much time. Her hands would lose their dexterity in only a few minutes in the winter night air at this altitude.

The bow line dangled and whipped uselessly in the whirlwind between the two ships, already beginning to unravel. Somehow it had snapped, and she could only be thankful this calamity had been over the great island, and not one inhabited by pirates. She waved at Freddie, who moved aft to release the swing and let her down.

Daisy's entire being focused on the dancing length of rope. Gently, she moved her feet to adjust for the blast of the wind. Luckily, it was blowing her straight toward her goal.

Careful … careful …

One hand gripping the rope of the swing, she leaned out over hundreds of feet of cold air and grabbed it. "Got you!"

Instead of reeling her up and risking her losing hold of it, William gently brought the conveyance lower while the swing rose and locked into place. With swift movements, she knotted the rope around both of the iron supports that had once been steps, and wove the raveled tail end through the ironwork pattern of the swing for good measure.

She stared at it, finally realizing what the pattern was that Tobin had welded into his creation. Feathers. Flight.

How very clever and kind of him. She wondered that she hadn't seen it before.

She scrambled through the rear door and locked it down. "All secure, William," she called. "Let's go home."

Victoria
8:00 p.m.

The conveyance landed with a bump and lifted again, the weight and buoyancy of number five carrying it a few feet across the airfield.

Davey saw at once that he must tie her down, or they would bounce right into one of the other ships—and after all they had gone through to steal them, he wasn't about to let that happen. He let down the gangway and ran out, straight into Daisy's arms.

She was weeping with joy and he hugged her as hard as he could before both of them said, "The ropes!"

But several aeronauts already on the field had seen them land, and before you could say Jack Robinson, number five was safely moored alongside the conveyance.

Didn't the airfield look properly full now!

And then it was all he could do to breathe as William and Freddie hugged him and Daisy covered whatever bit of his face she could reach with kisses.

"We had such a fright when Jake told us—"

"It was a bullet, I'm sure of it—"

"Oh, Davey, how brave and clever you were to set her going in circles!"

"I was, rather, wasn't I?" He grinned as William ruffled his hair. "Where is Jake? He's brought all four ships in. And Jenny and Sootie? They were in number three. Are they all right?"

"Jenny and Sootie?" Daisy repeated, laughing. "Have you been collecting animals as well as airships?"

"Jenny is a *girl*," Davey told her indignantly. "She was at the vanes of number three, ahead of me. Pig Iron Kelly's personal flagship. The pirates kidnapped her and killed her parents and when they were going to kill her hen for the shindig, I told her she ought to come with us. So she did."

"Miss Jenny is quite all right," said one of the aeronauts. "She and Mr. Fletcher are in the mess hall having something to eat. Pig Iron Kelly's flagship, eh?"

"Yes, that one there." Davey pointed at the largest.

"We'd better have a closer look," the aeronaut said to his companion. "Who knows what treasures we'll find that will help us ahead of the attack tomorrow."

"Oh, I don't think they're going to attack," Davey said, doing his best to sound modest. "I blew up the house where they were having a council of war. At least fifty of them were inside it."

"Yes, we saw," William said dryly. "The entire city saw. It is also likely that all of Port Townsend saw."

"I meant *our* attack," the aeronaut informed him with a grin. "Strike while the iron is hot, as my dad always says. As soon as we make certain these vessels are flightworthy, we're running up proper colors and paying a call on whoever is left."

"The inspector hopes that tomorrow will see the end of the pirate problem in the archipelago," the other one told them. "Now, run along. Your friends will be wanting to know you're alive and well."

They found Jake and Jenny, with Sootie in her lap, in the mess hall, regaling Inspector Kent, Professor Linden, and the assembled aeronauts with the story of their escape with the five airships.

"And here is my brother now," Jake said, rising to pull Davey into a bear hug. He said into Davey's hair, "I've never been so glad to see anyone in my life, and that's saying something."

"Me too," Davey said into his shirt, his arms around his waist. "I tried to think of what you would do, and sent the ship in circles until William and Daisy and Freddie found me."

"Wait …" Daisy looked from one to the other. "Whose brother?"

"While we were hiding in a fuselage, we discovered we share a dad," Jake said, an arm still companionably around Davey's shoulders. "Gil Fletcher left after my mother died, and met Davey's mother in Chicago."

"You don't say." William's eyebrows had risen into the curls on his forehead. "Half brothers, truly?"

"We think so," Jake said. "Best news I've had since my Maggie agreed to let me court her, innit?"

There was a commotion at the door, and in came Mrs Birch and Oscar Kent. Freddie made a sound in her throat as though someone had poked her. Oscar was dressed merely in his uniform trousers and a khaki shirt, as though he had leaped from his sick bed as soon as he had seen the conveyance set down, and barely managed to remember his boots.

"I couldn't keep him in bed," Mrs Birch said apologetically. "Not without tying him down."

Oscar looked dreadful—the bruises the pirates had given him had reached the purple-turning-to-green stage. And he limped, as though his ankle hurt, too. But the knock on the head didn't seem to be bothering him as he hauled Davey in for a hug.

"I was so worried when Dad told us what happened. And then the explosion—"

"I dropped a couple of Californio bombs down the chimney," Davey told him eagerly. "Me and Jake found a whole cabinet full of arms on one of the ships."

But Oscar, it seemed, wasn't as interested in bombs as Davey was. He let go of Davey and was looking at Freddie as if she were the sunrise after a storm.

And then it was she who was being gathered into his arms, as he murmured, "Thank heaven you're all right."

Davey caught Jake's eye and rolled his own. His brother grinned. "How about that jacket, mate?"

The ring!

Davey pulled off his filthy wool jacket and snapped the arm of it into a kind of chute. And down came the ring, diamond first, poking through the raggedy hole between sleeve and shoulder just enough for Davey to capture it in fingers that seemed far too grubby to be holding something so fine.

"Oscar?" he said. "You can have this back now."

Oscar turned, one arm still about Freddie, who had not made a single protest or stepped away or even blushed over being embraced in public in front of two dozen aeronauts. She pressed against his side as if she belonged there.

"Bless you for keeping it safe," Oscar said hoarsely. "I can never repay you."

"Oh, I'll think of something," Davey said cheerfully. But before he could go on and enumerate any number of ways his friend could do so, Oscar had turned, the ring in his fingers, to the Professor.

"Sir," he said, "I would like permission to ask for your daughter's hand."

Papa's eyebrows rose, and he tipped back his head in a hearty laugh. "Corporal, this is hardly the moment."

"I have not a moment to lose, sir." Oscar looked as fierce as any pirate, and the bruises only added to the effect.

But the Professor only smiled. "Frederica needs no permission from me, but if you do, you have it, and gladly."

Oscar released Freddie and sank down awkwardly on his good knee in front of her.

"Frederica," he said, "I never again want to live through a day like this one, not knowing if you were alive or dead, or ever coming back. I know I'm older than you, and we haven't known each other long, but I believe we have made up for in depth what our acquaintance has lacked in length."

Freddie's eyes filled with tears, and she began to tremble.

Oscar held up the ring, and its large square-cut diamond glittered in the electricks of the mess hall. "Frederica Rose Linden, will you do me the honor of becoming my wife?"

Davey agreed with the Professor—proposals were supposed to be romantic, with flowers. In a garden, maybe. Certainly private. If he were going to propose to a girl, that would be how he'd do it. Not in an aeronauts' mess, with all these men smiling and elbowing one another, and a pair of future fathers-in-law witnessing the whole affair.

But Freddie didn't seem to see any of these things. She only seemed to see Oscar.

"Yes," she said, in a voice that only trembled a little. "I will."

And then they were both crying, and the men were cheering, and Oscar was sliding the diamond on to her finger, and Mrs Birch was exclaiming, "Oh my dears, could you not have waited for a private moment?" and nobody was listening because Oscar was kissing Freddie and Davey was quite certain she was kissing him back.

Davey looked away to give them some privacy and saw Jenny sneak a big piece of her biscuit off her plate and on to the bench next to her, where Sootie was now perched. The biscuit vanished as though by magic, after which the hen blinked contentedly in perfect innocence, having not left so much as a crumb at the scene of the crime. His eyes met Jenny's, and she grinned.

At which point Davey realized he had never been so hungry in all his life. People could get engaged and make spectacles of themselves if they wanted. He was going to sit on Sootie's other side and have a good dinner.

It had been a hard day's work, and he deserved it.

CHAPTER 17

VICTORIA

January 16, 1896
8:50 a.m.

Freddie balanced Oscar's breakfast tray on one hip and knocked softly upon his door. Technically, it was Jake's door, but he had been perfectly content to share Davey's room, and Mrs Birch had produced a pair of hand-stitched quilts for the parlor sofa for Jenny. The girl was still fast asleep despite the rattle of pots and breakfast china in the kitchen. The little black hen had perched on the carved wood arabesque on the back of the sofa, for all the world as though she was keeping watch.

Freddie distinctly remembered her being put in the garden shed the night before, while Jenny had unwillingly gone into a hot bath and been scrubbed within an inch of her life. But squaring that with Mrs Birch was Jenny's nevermind, not hers.

Softly, she opened Oscar's door and went in. Clementine was sitting on the edge of the bed, gazing into her son's poor

196

abused face as he slept. She turned as Freddie put the tray on the night table, where the scent of coffee filled the room. Freddie had made him toast and honey, and a pair of coddled eggs. Mrs Birch had added a fat slice of ham. In her opinion, a breakfast without some sort of meat in it was no breakfast for a man at all.

Clementine's gaze fell upon her diamond ring on Freddie's finger, and her misty hand went to her throat.

Are you engaged? Truly?

Freddie nodded, and said in a whisper, "I hope you approve."

Oh, yes. She covered her heart with both hands, then opened them out to Freddie. *I love you already.*

Freddie's lips trembled, and she blinked back the sudden welling of tears. "I wish—"

But Clementine only shook her head. *For as long as I am here, we will be a family.*

A tremulous smile bloomed on Freddie's lips, and she nodded. Family. Think of it! She would have two families now —good and brave people, including the deceased ones. It didn't matter in the least that her future mother-in-law was a ghost. They would love one another regardless.

"Now, here is a sight to wake up to." Oscar gazed at her, love blazing in his eyes, even if one was still swollen.

"Good morning." She touched his forehead, pretending to feel for his temperature so she would not lean in and kiss him in front of his mother, and settled into her usual chair.

"I had the strangest dream," he said, his voice rough with sleep. "I dreamed I saw my mother, sitting right here on the bed." He patted the coverlet, his hand passing through Clementine's knee. "You showed her your ring."

"I did," she said. "She is still here. And she is so pleased."

He gazed at her. "You are mocking me. Is that any way to behave to your newly minted fiancé?"

But she did not smile in return. "Oscar, I must tell you something." She took his hand. "No mockery, only truth."

"As long as you have not changed your mind about marrying me, I can hear anything you wish to say with equanimity."

"I have not, nor will I, change my mind," she said softly. "But if *you* do, I will not hold it against you. You remember my saying that I was something of a medium?"

"Yes." His gaze was intense. Clementine leaned forward in interest.

"That was … a fib. Or at least, not the entire truth."

"And what is the truth, dear?" He flushed. "I'm sorry, that just came out."

How difficult it was not to kiss him! "You may call me *dear* a hundred times a day and I will not tire of it," she told him softly. "But now you must listen. The truth is that …" She must say the words she had fallen asleep rehearsing. He must know everything now, before their engagement went any further. "I see the dead. Sometimes they communicate with me, sometimes I only feel their grief and rage. Many times they wish me to pass messages to their loved ones. Which I cannot do, for who would believe it? The living would think me mad."

He did not speak. Neither did Clementine. She only reached out to touch his hand. His fingers moved and lay still.

"In Port Townsend, you may recall, we also solved the first murder."

"Yes?" He looked confused at the swerve in her story.

"But it was not only because of our inquiries. It was because the victim appeared to me herself. The window in the bedroom we were staying in, you see, was the one from which she had been pushed."

Understanding began to dawn.

"And the fainting spells of the culprit, after our capture? Those were simply fright. One of the warriors from the Chemakum village accompanied us. He has a masterful talent for frightening people into insensibility."

"I wish I had been able to thank him," Oscar said in a wondering tone. "But perhaps he heard me. Perhaps they all did, as we passed out of the mist that last time."

It took a moment for the significance of this to sink in.

Clementine touched his hand, and he turned it palm up, where her fingers lay mistily in his.

"It seems I no longer have to pretend, either," he said. "But you must not tell Father. He has a very practical turn of mind that does not allow for … other possibilities in the world. Let him suppose you a medium. He will accept in you what he would never accept in me."

Freddie could not quite believe it. "You mean—you—" She turned to Clementine. "He can see you, too?"

She tilted her head from side to side. *In a manner of speaking.*

"Why did you never tell me?"

"Why did you not tell me?" he tossed back at her. "For the same reasons, I suspect. I have not your gift, which I first suspected that evening, when you asked permission of the guardians in the village to allow me through. Such a sight you were! If I had not already fallen in love, that moment would have sealed my fate. No, mine is limited to … feelings. A knowledge, I suppose you might say. I can feel Mother's presence, and once in a great while, when he really tries, that of my uncle Montrose as well. Usually out in the garden. It was his pride and joy."

"Montrose. Our Mrs Birch's late husband?"

"Yes. Mother's brother. But I cannot see them in the way it seems you can. Only now and again, in a dream that is not a dream, can I see Mother clearly. But even that is a gift I gladly accept."

Freddie felt a little winded. "Then ... you do not mind? You do not wish to break off our engagement?"

"Darling girl." He splayed his fingers and entwined them with hers. "Of all the people in the world, it seems a miracle that we found each other. You need not fear that I will betray your secret. But I admit I am relieved that we may talk freely of such things in the bosom of your family. Speaking of which, I was pleased that my grandfather's clothes fit your papa so well."

Clementine looked very wise. One ghostly brow rose.

Freddie had to laugh. "You may thank your mama for that. And I noticed that Mrs Birch noticed, too," she said to Clementine. "But we are not to play matchmaker, dear Mrs Kent. Poor Papa has only just found his own children. We must give him a little time to remember how to be a father before we suggest his being a husband again."

But Clementine made no promises.

When Freddie shared the coddled eggs and toast with her son, she did not bat an eye. But when Freddie finally lost the battle and leaned down to kiss him before she took the tray downstairs, Clementine melted through the wall and departed.

"She is gone," Freddie said with a smile.

"My mother, the soul of discretion." Oscar sighed. "You're not going already?"

"I am." Freddie got herself to the door before she found the whole morning whiled away in his company. "The newly designated RCAP ships will be returning soon. If you want to see them flying their new colors, and hear all about the mission, you must get up and make yourself presentable."

"May I escort you to the field?"

"If you do not, I shall weep for days."

He flung back the coverlet with energy. Laughing, Freddie escaped out the door before she saw anything an unmarried young lady shouldn't.

10:40 a.m.

The fractious wind of the night before had blown the clouds out to sea, so the assembly on the RCAP field could see the returning ships from quite a distance. Her Majesty's Union Jack fluttered proudly from the shrouds at the stern of each gondola, making it easier, Daisy suspected, for the aeronauts to tell whose ship was whose if it came to a pitched air battle.

They had departed at dawn to meet Pig Iron Kelly's attack, should there be one. But it was now midmorning and no one had had word that any such thing had happened. Daisy shifted from foot to foot, as anxious to hear as any of the newspaper reporters among their number could be.

A little distance away, Davey and Jenny supervised Sootie's hunting in the grass. Mrs Birch had rather pointedly suggested that Sootie might be more comfortable in the garden, behind the picket fence, but Jenny was adamant that they should not be separated. Daisy had a feeling that the bird's sojourn in the shed had frightened the girl somehow. Perhaps, as Davey said, she did not yet trust that Sootie would not end up in the soup pot. Daisy had seen her with a kitchen rag, discreetly cleaning up after Sootie, so as not to ruffle Mrs Birch's feathers further.

"Here they come!" Papa said as the ships sank into their final approach, one after the other.

"I cannot wait to hear about the battle," William said, shading his eyes against the sun.

Inspector Kent himself, they had learned from the ground crew, was at the helm of Pig Iron Kelly's flagship. Had it been Daisy, she would have done so to spit in the eye of the man who had owned it. But Inspector Kent was surely more noble than she. William had told her how badly the pirates had treated poor Oscar once they'd found out that not only was he an RCAP aeronaut, but the son of the man their leader hated most in the world. Daisy rather felt it was fitting that Oscar's father should wreak his own havoc on the pirates in revenge.

The ships settled gracefully on the field in perfect formation, fanning out from the flagship in a *V*, the way the geese flew in their skeins in the autumn. Perhaps it was not the most efficient use of space, but goodness, it did look fine! The man with the daguerreotype camera had already exposed his first plate, and she regretted that she had left her sketchbook at the boarding house. She must simply commit the wonderful sight to memory, and remember that the shadows ought to be Prussian Blue, not merely Payne's Gray with Lamp Black added.

Inspector Kent and his crews disembarked, and waved the

welcoming party into the headquarters building. "I shall give our report once," he announced, "to colleagues and newspapermen alike. Come along into the mess hall. My captains and I will be brief."

"Oh, I hope not," William murmured. "We shall have to extract the most exciting details from him at dinner."

"And after a suitable interval, they will appear in *Tales of a Medicine Man?*" Daisy was beginning to enjoy the fact that her fiancé was the author of the newspaper column read by half the continent—though lately, the similarities to their own adventures were enough to make her blush.

"My lips are sealed," William said, and then stole a kiss to prove it.

Talk and laughter built to a roar in the mess hall until Inspector Kent and his four captains took their places at the front of the room. The newspaper men tried to shout questions—

And newspaper women too—

"Good heavens," Daisy said. "There is Elizabeth Selkirk— and Maylene Willamette beside her! What are they doing here? I thought Beth to be in Reno by now with Edward Bonnell, choosing her trousseau."

"Elizabeth must be reporting for her paper," William said. "And didn't you tell me Miss Willamette's dream was to start her own magazine? It seems I may have some competition."

"Thank you for your attention." Inspector Kent had no need of a speaking horn; his voice carried quite clearly over the heads of his audience. "You will all have seen the explosion on San Juan Island last night."

"What caused it, sir?" Elizabeth asked in clear tones, her

own natural authority coming to the fore in a way Daisy had rarely seen permitted back in Bodie.

"From the evidence at the scene, it appeared Pig Iron Kelly stored a large quantity of gunpowder in the cellars of his headquarters on each island. In this instance, perhaps a flying spark from the firebox in the boiler, perhaps a dropped cigar—in any case, the gunpowder ignited and demolished not only the house, but everything within about twenty yards."

Elizabeth and Maylene both scribbled furiously in small notebooks.

Davey and Jake looked at one another, then Jake whispered something to the dismayed boy. Daisy wondered if Inspector Kent was keeping Davey's part in it out of the public eye for his own good.

"How did you come by the pirate airships?" someone else demanded.

"Through the great bravery and skill of two individuals who were working incognito for the RCAP in the archipelago," Inspector Kent said. "Their names will not be released just yet. But they are to have the credit for the chain of events that led to this morning's complete victory."

Now Jake and Davey exchanged grins. So they were to be acknowledged. It was only the details that the RCAP would keep quiet.

"Are they present, sir?" the reporter persisted.

"I cannot say." The inspector was becoming impatient.

"Hip hip, hurrah!" someone shouted. "Three cheers for our two brave aeronauts!"

The mess hall erupted in cheers, and Davey danced from one foot to the other, hugging himself with glee. Jake seized him in a one-armed squeeze while the wave of cheering washed over them.

Daisy was quite sure the inspector was fighting a smile before he cleared his throat and lifted a hand for silence once more.

"We lifted this morning at dawn, having received information that Pig Iron Kelly intended to attack our fair city. We did meet some resistance. There were two ships in particular, one lifting from the island of the salt springs and one moored on Saturna, who attempted to engage, but they were swiftly routed and went down, one in the strait and one on a small, rocky islet close by."

"Were there survivors?" a reporter called.

"No. They were holed too badly. The descent was so swift as to preclude anyone's being able to walk away."

Silence fell as the assembly imagined the scene.

"Our next objective was to ascertain whether the four ships we had heard of on Horcasitas Island were going to engage. When we were within sight, we observed there were only three. One had fled, and the remaining vessels were captured by the men of our detachment at Port Townsend in a simultaneous attack, while we provided a distraction as we came into view."

Cheers from the audience. Daisy had to admire the inspector—when he mounted a defense, he left nothing to chance.

"So may we safely say that the archipelago is free once more?" Elizabeth Selkirk asked, her pencil poised over her notebook.

"There will be a cleanup operation mounted, of course," Inspector Kent allowed. "Kelly had seven islands under his control, and many more had been coerced into subjection by the raids of his men. It may take some weeks to bring the remaining pirates to justice. But you may be sure that we shall see it played out to the end. And then the inhabitants of the islands, both subjects of Her Majesty and those of the original nations, will be able to return to their homes and villages and take up their lives without let or hindrance."

"Will the headwoman of these nations, Malina Chalmers, presently in residence in Port Townsend, be involved, sir?" Elizabeth asked.

"Yes, of course," Inspector Kent said. "We are fortunate to enjoy an excellent relationship with her and her fleet. Thank you all for your attendance. My remarks are concluded."

A babble of questions went up, but the inspector was distracted by a constable who had crept to his side with a slip of paper. He read it and looked up.

The reporters came to attention, pencils poised.

"I have just been notified that the Duke and Duchess of Cornwall left Edmonton this morning under full escort, which included the vessel of Sir Ian and Lady Hollys and our six RCAP airships. If the winds are favorable, they will arrive tomorrow at noon following an overnight visit to the spa and hot springs in the mountains."

Another roar of questions went up, but Inspector Kent had lost his patience. Signaling his sergeants, he strode from the mess hall.

"I wonder how many ships are to be squeezed on to the airfield now?" Daisy murmured to her father, standing on her other side.

"It sounds like quite a number," he said. "William, perhaps

Davey and Jake and I might move the conveyance immediately back to its place in the orchard?"

"Thank you, sir. That's very thoughtful of you."

And clever, too, Daisy thought. Better to employ Davey in a task he enjoyed, in case he could not contain himself and undid all the inspector's good work by buttonholing a reporter.

In fact, she intended to do the buttonholing herself.

As her father rounded up the two young heroes of the hour, Daisy slipped through the crowd and seized the arms of the only two ladies in the press corps.

"Here is a delightful surprise!" she said, pulling them into a hug. "Why did you not tell us?"

Elizabeth laughed. "For the simple reason that a forwarding address of *Victoria* does not allow for correspondence. And then when we heard that Corporal Kent's ship had been shot down, it was all too easy to fear that the conveyance had gone down with it."

"I am very glad that it did not," Maylene said shyly. "I hope there is a marvelous story attached to the experience."

"Some stories are better left to the imagination, and some are fit only for the *Tales of a Medicine Man*. Come. William and Freddie will be delighted to see you."

They were, their farewell on the beach at the Chemakum village still glowing in their minds.

"But you must excuse me," Elizabeth said. "I must file my story at once or my editor will make me reimburse the steamer fare he paid to get me here. It was a stroke of luck that he had no one else to send, but that does not make him any less tight-fisted about it."

Daisy swallowed her questions about the whereabouts of

Edward Bonnell, who at last sight could not be parted from Elizabeth. "Come home with us. There is plenty of paper and ink, and you will likely be able to borrow a pigeon from the RCAP. They have an abundance of them at the moment."

With Elizabeth holed up in Mrs Birch's office, scribbling furiously, Daisy introduced Maylene Willamette to Freddie and William, and then to Mrs Birch. Jenny had gone with Papa, Jake, and Davey, presumably taking the little hen with her.

Mrs Birch asked, "Where are you young ladies staying? For with the royal visit, I cannot imagine there is so much as a garret to be had in the entire city."

"You are quite right," Maylene said. "I am afraid that we have not had time to find somewhere. Do you have a recommendation?"

Daisy and Freddie turned beseeching gazes upon their hostess.

Mrs Birch laughed. "Most of my rooms are at present occupied, but on the floor above I have, not a garret, but a couple of rooms for single persons. My rates are very reasonable, and to be honest, if you are friends of the Lindens, then I would prefer you as guests over anyone. Even if by dinnertime I may charge a king's ransom and be assured of getting it."

"How kind you are," Maylene said gratefully. "When Elizabeth goes to file her story, I will stop by the steamship office and collect our valises."

Daisy drew her into the parlor as Mrs Birch bustled upstairs to be certain the rooms were ready for guests. "From the sounds in the kitchen, I would guess that the estimable Mr Harrow is already preparing tea."

Oscar offered her a chair and returned to the sofa next to Freddie. "Miss Willamette, I am astounded to see you, of all people, here. Have you taken up the newspaper business as well?"

The young woman's mouth firmed. "I have taken up my *life*, Corporal." She glanced at Daisy. "As a result of a certain conversation, I decided that the last day under my mother's thumb could not come soon enough. I took Daisy's advice and offered my friendship to Miss Selkirk, who welcomed me into her circle with a warmth I did not deserve."

"I am sure that is not true," Daisy chided her. "And we have seen the proof of it."

"She and her fiancé are going to found a magazine, you see. And they wish me to have the editor's position."

"Editor!" Freddie repeated.

"Fiancé!" Daisy exclaimed. "Where *is* Mr Bonnell?"

"In Port Townsend, still, attending to the final details before they move."

"To Reno?"

"No indeed." Maylene looked bemused. "They have received such an offer from a railroad baron for the house there that it could not be refused. They plan to make their home here, and establish the magazine by spring. Besides, Edward says the soil is much better here for gardening. He can hardly wait to purchase property and begin. He will have a separate premises for the printing press and the offices, including mine."

Daisy clapped her hands in delight. "How wonderful! We plan the same. Not to plant gardens or found magazines, I mean, but to make our home here. We shall have a ready-made circle of friends. I am so pleased!"

"Daisy—" Papa began. Frowned. Lifted his head to meet her eyes. "I am afraid the position at the university no longer exists. I do not, in fact, have a reason to stay."

"Other than Freddie and Oscar and William and I, Papa," Daisy said, reproach in her tone. "Surely you cannot wish to go back to Bath. Or Edinburgh."

"No indeed. But I cannot merely—" He stopped as Mrs Birch rustled in from the stairs and Mr Harrow wheeled in a tea cart that nearly groaned with its delicious burden.

Daisy would have given a lot to know how her father had meant to conclude that sentence.

CHAPTER 18

VICTORIA

January 17, 1896
Noon

The entire city seemed to have turned out to welcome the royal couple to their shores. Streets and gardens for blocks around the airfield were clogged with cheering people waving Union Jacks—for the landing was not to be at the civic airfield, but at the RCAP field, close to the offices of the Columbia Territory's government officials now descending the steps to welcome them.

"We should have gone up on the roof, like the Professor said," Davey grumbled. "We won't be able to see a thing once they moor."

The inhabitants of Mrs Birch's boarding house were crowded into the front garden. Daisy had thought they would have a splendid view, but she had not counted on the crowds clogging the street in front. They would be lucky if the picket fence were not knocked down. At this rate, Davey would soon

211

be charging a nickel so that perfect strangers might go up on the widow's walk with him.

That morning's paper, *The Daily Colonist*, had been effusive about the social whirl in Edmonton the week before the royal couple's departure. Balls, teas, reviews of the RCAP and Her Majesty's armed forces, as well as hunting parties and even a description of the mountain spa had been reported on at such length it filled nearly two pages, complete with engravings. The newspaper had concluded,

And now Their Royal Highnesses are to bid farewell to the Northern Light and ascend to the Jewel of the Pacific, where the climate is salubrious and the company more so. Sir James Dunsmuir, Inspector Marcus Kent of the RCAP, and Dean and Mrs Bodey of the University will welcome the royal couple at the RCAP airfield at noon sharp. Following the Duke's remarks, the party will proceed by steam landau directly to Cary Castle.

A grand ball to which all the notables of our city have been invited is to take place there this evening. We wish the royal couple the very best of visits, and hope the hospitality of our city conveys our joy at their coming.

Elizabeth Selkirk and Maylene Willamette were somewhere in the press area on the airfield. Daisy had just said to William, "I doubt we shall see much of them today," when a mighty cheer went up. Word ran through the crowd that the royal airship had just been spotted.

A constable pushed through the throng and waved at Mrs Birch. "Begging your pardon, ma'am, but Inspector Kent sent me to escort you and your guests to the stands. He's got a block of seats secured for you."

"Oh, bless him," Mrs Birch said. "I knew we could count on Marcus. Come along, all of you, before they moor and we miss everything."

Daisy took Jenny's hand. This morning she had listened to reason and put Sootie in a tall, roomy birdcage that Mrs Birch, aghast at the sight of the hen walking freely about the house, had hastily located for her. Freddie and Oscar slipped out of the gate, but not before Papa had offered his arm to Mrs Birch, who accepted it with a smile before she tilted her parasol up against the sun.

"I'm going to join the ground crew for *Swan*," Jake said to Davey. "Want to come?"

A glance at William and Daisy secured permission, and he scampered off with his brother, who wore his navigator's uniform so he would not be stopped at the roped-off perimeter of the field.

"I wonder if Davey realizes he is at a crossroads in his life?" William murmured to Daisy as they followed the constable across the grass. The former pirate ships had been moored at the civic field to make room for the royal party … and to prevent any alarm among the RCAP crews who might not have been briefed about the presence of so many forbidding grey ships.

"What do you mean, dearest?"

"Only that Jake will be lifting with *Swan* when it goes, while we remain here." He peered around Daisy to Jenny, walking beside them in a watchful silence. "*We* meaning you as well, Jenny. You have a home with us, wherever that might be, never fear."

Jenny's shoulders seemed to relax, and Daisy squeezed her hand with a smile. "And Sootie. We would never forget her.

Once we are settled, we can turn our minds to locating members of your family, but until then, we will stay together."

But Daisy had not thought beyond the miracle of Davey's having actual living family to consider what the boy might want to do now that he knew he had a brother. "You don't think he will want to go with Jake, do you? As Lin did with her cousin? After all we have been through together? Why, we are as close to family as Davey has come since his mother died."

"I agree, and to be honest, I think he feels that way, too."

"He does," Jenny ventured.

"Has he spoken with you about it?" William asked.

"No," the girl admitted. "But he hasn't said he wants to go away in *Swan*, either. Daisy, what if I did have family?"

They were nearly at the stands, which were filling rapidly now that the ships could be seen in the distance. The roars of the crowd increased.

"Do you remember anyone, dear?" Daisy said as the constable directed them up a set of rickety steps. "Aunts or uncles? Grandparents?" Had Jenny even told them her last name? Daisy tried to remember, but it was difficult with all the excitement and the noise.

"I think I have grandparents," she said doubtfully. "I haven't seen them for a long time. Papa's father was a teacher."

"Then we shall begin there," William said. "But for now, let's get into our seats. Freddie is waving as though she thinks we will be swallowed up out here, and I agree with her."

They were barely in their seats when the dignitaries paced down the marble steps of the headquarters building to the chairs that had been set out on the grass. The royal airship— its crest of the lion and unicorn rampant emblazoned on its massive fuselage—made a pass over the airfield. Out as far as the harbor it went, to a cacophony of horns and klaxons of the steamships and sailing vessels moored there, then back around in a circle for its final approach. *Swan* sailed close in its wake, and here came all six of Victoria's RCAP vessels, fanning out behind it for maximum effect.

Wide-eyed, Jenny bounced in her seat and clapped her hands. "Oh, isn't it a spectacle!"

Daisy had never seen anything like it, either. But then, she and Freddie, unlike the Hollys and their friends, did not move in royal or even noble circles. At least they were in the stands, and so close to the welcoming committee they would not even need the speaking horns to hear the official greetings. They could dine out on this experience for years—to say nothing of the letter she could write to Aunt Jane.

The ground crews ran forward, and the ships were moored. And at last the royal gangway lowered and Daisy had her first glimpse of the Queen's grandson, second in line to the throne, and his wife.

"Look at that dress!" Freddie moaned in delight.

"How beautiful she is," Jenny said.

The Duchess was dressed, not in a traveling costume, but in a fur-trimmed blue velvet jacket over an afternoon gown that positively frothed with ruffled lace. Her high collar was encircled with not one, not two, but three magnificent pearl necklaces, and she carried herself with an uprightness that belied the S-curve of her very fashionable corset.

Beside her, one hardly saw the Duke, with his pointed beard and mustache, wearing the uniform of a Commander of the Royal Aeronautic Corps.

A contingent of constables escorted them to the gathered

notables, where Sir James bowed deeply and welcomed them at some length. Inspector Kent bowed and accepted their thanks for their escort. And then Papa shifted in his seat as Dean Bodey advanced to bow and clear his throat in preparation for his speech.

Into the restless silence—Daisy quite agreed, fewer speeches were in order if the royal couple were to stroll about and greet the Queen's subjects in her name—someone exclaimed, "Is that my grandpapa?"

Daisy started. She could have sworn that had been—

"Grandpapa!" Jenny leaped from her seat and climbed over several sets of knees between her and the steps.

"Jenny!" William called. "Where are you—"

Dean Bodey launched into his remarks as her shabby, too-thin figure dashed across the grass. One of the constables in the honor guard lunged to grab her, but she had not lived with pirates for five years without learning how to evade capture.

"Grandpapa!"

Dean Bodey lost his place and the royal couple turned in astonishment as Jenny dodged around them and flung herself at the Dean of the University.

He caught her as she quite disappeared within his billowing academic robes. "Who— Is that— Jennifer?" His voice cracked. "Jennifer, can it really be—?"

Quite forgetting the Duke and Duchess, who gaped at the scene as unselfconsciously as Daisy herself, he dropped to his knees to envelop the weeping girl in his arms.

Mrs Bodey broke from the ranks of the receiving line to haul up her skirts and run to join them. "Jenny! Can it be true?

Where have you come from? Oh, my darling girl, we thought you were dead!"

Jenny went into her grandmother's arms, burying her neatly braided head in her breast. Somehow the Dean got himself to his feet and remembered where he was.

"Your Royal Highnesses … I'm so sorry. I— Good heavens." He took a deep breath. "My son's ship was shot down by pirates five years ago and we thought all aboard had been killed. I do not understand—I—I— Professor Linden?"

Daisy realized belatedly that her father had left his seat and was now joining the disarray. He bowed to the bemused royal couple and turned to the Dean.

"Jenny was rescued by Sir Ian and Lady Hollys's navigator and my daughter's ward," he said gently. "She has been staying with us across the way, at the home of Inspector Kent's sister-in-law. Had we known she was a member of your family, sir, we would have restored her to you instantly."

"The Hollys' navigator? Your daughter's ward?" He repeated the words as though doing so would help him understand.

"She has been imprisoned on San Juan for some time. She came back with our friends on the stolen pirate vessels, right after the explosion we saw from Cary Castle."

"Your … your family, it seems, has done an incalculable service for us. After I gave your post away to someone else, too."

"Stolen pirate vessels?" The Duke abandoned protocol altogether in his interest. "I say, how fascinating."

"I'm so sorry, Your Royal Highness," the Dean said, smoothing Jenny's hair as though he could hardly believe she was there and real. "Please excuse us. You will wish to make your speech."

"I certainly don't," he retorted. "What I wish for is a good stiff drink, but failing that, my wife and I will greet the people who have been so kind as to come out to welcome us."

He waved, she waved, the crowd roared, and then he turned back. "There. Now, what's this about giving away this man's post?"

Papa said, "Sir, with all due respect, that is neither here nor there. What matters is that Jenny has found her family."

"With the help, apparently, of yours."

"Well, yes, but it has nothing to do with the post. Do excuse me. I have intruded long enough. I only wanted to see Jenny safe in all this crowd."

The Duke looked from Papa to the Dean. "I say, Dean, have this man and his family been invited to Dunsmuir's do this evening?"

"I—what? I haven't any idea."

"Forgive me, Your Royal Highness, but no." Sir James had finally found his tongue.

"Well, why bloody not? It seems we have something to celebrate. I want to meet this navigator. And this ward. See that they come, will you? Now may I please get my bride out of this cold? And where is that drink?"

As though he had planned it that way all along, Inspector Kent escorted the royal couple past the gaping receiving line and into the landaus waiting in the drive. The crowd surged toward the harbor to follow their route. The stands emptied with dizzying speed.

In ten minutes the only ones left were Daisy and William, Freddie and Oscar, and Mrs Birch, sitting in their places in the stands, still frozen in astonishment. Jake and Davey were nowhere to be seen, and Jenny had gone with the Bodeys. At least, so Daisy assumed.

Papa climbed up to fetch them. "Are you going to sit here all afternoon? For if I am not mistaken, we have all been invited to a ball."

"I—I— What just happened?" Daisy finally managed.

Her father gazed down at her, and the corners of his mouth twitched. "A girl has found her family, a man has asked for a drink, and a boy will have to find a new suit of clothes."

"So, nothing out of the ordinary, then," William said.

"Not for this family," Freddie said.

"Mrs Birch," Papa said to her with a courtly bow, "will you do me the honor of attending the Duke and Duchess of Cornwall's ball with me?"

Mrs Birch dragged her gaze away from the crowds pursuing the royal couple. "After today, Professor," she said, "I should never dream of refusing you anything."

A roar of rage that turned into a scream brought them to their feet in alarm.

"Jenny!" Daisy picked up her skirts and flew down the stairs, then dashed across the grass to a landau where a struggling figure fought and kicked. "Jenny, what is the matter?" She prepared herself for battle lest the girl's happiness at seeing her grandparents had been utterly misplaced.

"Sootie!" Jenny roared, her face scarlet with fear and rage, tears running down her face. "They're taking me away without Sootie!"

"I haven't the least idea what she means." Mrs Bodey's hat was askew, and tears were swimming in her eyes, too. "She won't get in the landau."

"Sootie is my *hen!*" Jenny shouted. "I won't leave her!"

"Of course you won't, darling," Daisy said as though this were a given. "I wouldn't, either."

At her matter-of-fact tone, Jenny's fear began to dissipate a little, and she gulped back a sob.

Daisy turned to the couple. "Sootie is a very well behaved black hen who has been Jenny's only companion during her imprisonment. She saved the bird from being eaten by pirates moments before our ward helped her escape, so you can imagine their mutual attachment."

"Eaten by pirates!" Mrs Bodey leaned rather heavily on the bonnet of the landau.

"This bird is … a pet, then?" Poor Dean Bodey looked on the verge of a breakdown himself.

"Yes, as beloved as any dog or cat."

"More," Jenny said, stamping her foot.

"If you agree that they should not be parted, I will ask my fiancé to fetch Sootie and her traveling apparatus. She and Jenny may go with you comfortably in the rear of the landau."

"Traveling apparatus," the dean repeated feebly.

"Quite right," his wife told Daisy, visibly pulling herself together. "Of course they must not be parted."

"And you will not eat her?" Jenny demanded of her grandmother.

"No indeed." The woman looked shocked at the very suggestion. "That would be as great a sin as eating *you.*"

So the lady had a sense of humor, Daisy realized as their eyes met. And ten minutes later, Jenny meekly went with the couple, after many assurances that Daisy would bring Davey over to see her as soon as it could be arranged. Sootie and her tall cylinder of a birdcage rode in the rear, Jenny's arm about the cage in case they should hit a bump.

"Grandparents," William said in a wondering tone as they puttered around a corner and vanished. "A brother. Your long-lost papa. Never mind solving murders, Daisy. You ought to hang out your shingle as a finder of lost persons."

"I only found one of those three, and to be precise, Freddie saw Papa first." She took his arm. "The only person I am interested in finding at the moment is Davey. He is to go to this ball, too, and if he is to be made presentable enough to make his bows to royalty, there is no time to lose."

VICTORIA

1:50 p.m.

*L*ogic dictated that if Davey had gone with Jake, and Jake was navigator aboard *Swan*, then the first place one ought to look for him was the great blue and silver airship. Daisy collected Freddie and Oscar, and her father and Mrs Birch, and invited them along. The gangway was down, and a midshipman was posted there. He grinned when he saw them.

"Midshipman," Daisy greeted him as they strolled up. "We meet again."

"Miss Linden." The boy offered her a snappy salute. "Miss Freddie. If you're looking for Jake and Davey, they're with our Alice in the main saloon."

"Our Alice?" Papa murmured as they boarded.

"Lady Hollys," she whispered over her shoulder.

"Quite the informal crew, I see."

"Less a crew and more a family, I believe. Come, it has not

been so many months that Freddie and I have forgotten the way."

They found their missing ward in the saloon, as promised, and after a babble of greetings and introductions, the young man called Charlie brought in tea and two large trays of cakes and sandwiches. Then he leaned on a chair behind his captains to hear the interrupted tale of what their navigator had been up to during his shore leave.

When Jake had brought them all into the picture and revealed that Davey was his half-brother, Lady Hollys sat back on the sofa looking a little winded.

"Jake Fletcher," she said, shaking her head. "I ought to have known better than to leave you alone for two minutes."

"If he hadn't, milady, we'd never have found each other," Davey said earnestly. "And those guns wouldn't've been spiked, and the pirates would have attacked Victoria and—"

Lady Hollys laughed. "You're quite right. History is better this way. And you must call me Alice, as my friends do. 'Lady Hollys' always gives me a fright, in case Ian's mother has boarded *Swan* without my knowing."

"If you don't mind my asking … Alice … why were you not outside with all the dignitaries?" Daisy asked shyly. "The speeches were going along nicely until Jenny, the girl Davey rescued, interrupted them and everything fell into disarray."

"We're not really the dignitary sort," Alice said with a smile at her husband. "We had our share in Edmonton—no point in repeating it all. I would have liked to have seen this young lady set everything at sixes and sevens, though. I know a pair of girls who were capable of exactly the same at about that age."

"Is she all right?" Davey asked. "Did she really stop the Duke from making a speech?"

Papa laughed his booming laugh, and Daisy couldn't help but smile at the welcome sound. "He didn't seem to want to make a speech at all. He was more interested in a cold drink. I think our Jenny did him a favor."

"She has gone with her grandparents," Daisy said, "but we will be able to see her once the royal couple have departed and things settle down. Which brings me to the reason we came to find you, Davey," Daisy said. "You are to attend the ball this evening and be presented."

"You, too, Jake," William said. "The Duke wishes to thank you for your part in routing the pirates."

"Does he, now?" Jake's brows rose. "So much for our trying to keep that quiet. The papers will have a field day with it—two young men doing in one night what the RCAP has not been able to do for years."

"Now, now," Oscar said mildly. "Not sporting of you, old man. A good many chaps have given their lives trying, including Jenny's papa. And anyway, Dad presented it as being an undercover job. The RCAP is going to get the credit no matter how it comes out."

"Dad?" Sir Ian queried.

"My father, Inspector Marcus Kent," Oscar explained. "He is in charge of the headquarters detachment here."

"Ah, one of the dignitaries we saw." Sir Ian nodded.

"If you take my advice," Daisy said to Jake, "you'll offer the story to Elizabeth Selkirk as an exclusive. That way, you'll be certain it will be reported accurately." She paused. "If that is what you want."

"She's that friend of yours? The one from Bodie?" Jake

asked. Daisy nodded. "Maybe I will. Or maybe I won't. People might not like someone of my … reputation being presented to their Duke if all the facts were to come out. Maybe Davey and I should just keep the whole thing under our hats."

"But they already know about rescuing Jenny and stealing the ships," Davey pointed out. "We don't have to say anything about me dropping the bombs down the chimney. Or about you jumping out of the conveyance. Or about the guns."

"Probably best," Jake said with a nod.

Davey sat back. Clearly whatever his brother said was law.

Alice offered Papa the tray of iced cakes. He selected one with an image of *Swan* in blue on the top, and offered it to Mrs Birch before he took one of his own.

"I am very happy to see that you found your father, Daisy," Alice said. "The experience seems to have changed you, and I'm not speaking only of that ruby on your finger."

Daisy had to smile. "I am no longer that girl you met. Nor is Freddie." She glanced at her sister, who was pouring another cup of tea for Oscar. "Perhaps the biggest discovery we made is that friends are to be found everywhere. In each place we searched for Papa, we met people who not only helped us in our search, but who became the kind of friend one wants to go back to visit. We want to keep them in our lives." She touched Mrs Birch's hand. "The way the society of absent friends do. We would never have found Papa if it had not been for them, and the kind ladies of the Canton district in San Francisco de Assis, and Elizabeth Selkirk. We would likely have returned to Bath in despair."

"And I would have been hanged by now," Papa said.

Mrs Birch said, "Professor! Surely not."

"It is only too true. My girls and young William and Oscar

here saved my life in Port Townsend. Love drove my daughters across an ocean and a continent to find me. And love, I am happy to say, has found them in return."

Freddie leaned over to kiss Papa on the cheek, her eyes gleaming with sudden tears.

"So have you named the day?" Alice said to Daisy. "A big cathedral wedding, with eight bridesmaids, a choir, and a dress with a train so long you can make a tablecloth of it afterward?"

William burst out laughing. "Good heavens, I hope not."

Daisy couldn't help a smile. "To be honest, we have not thought any further than reaching Victoria. We have made no plans at all—except that Davey and Freddie and Oscar will stand up with us."

"Oh, yes," Freddie said.

"I will?" Oscar looked elated. "Delighted, of course. An honor."

"And it will *not* be in a cathedral."

"Ours was." Alice smiled affectionately at her husband, who picked up her hand and kissed her fingers. "A cathedral in a tiny Texican town in the mountains that had seen two hundred years of weddings. Only he and I, the padre, and his clerk for witness. It was perfect."

"That's the way to do it," Daisy said. "I just want the people I love around me. I don't particularly care where the occasion is held."

"Pity we couldn't do it this moment," William said, bumping her shoulder affectionately. "Everyone we care about is right here."

"Except Jenny," Davey objected.

"And Elizabeth," Freddie said. "Though I think she's back

at the boarding house, no doubt writing like a madwoman to file the story of the royal landing for her newspaper."

"If you'd like to, we have no objection," Alice said. "A ship-board wedding—just the thing, after all your adventures."

"What, aboard *Swan?*" Daisy laughed. "If only it were so easy."

"It is easy." Sir Ian straightened on the sofa. "We can do it right now, if you like. Not only am I co-captain of this vessel, I'm also a magistrate. We simply take her up as far as we like, enjoy the ceremony, and moor once more. Then we walk over there—" With his chin, he indicated the government offices. "—and register the marriage. After that, Charlie can rustle up a wedding supper, can't you, Charlie?"

"Of course, sir," the young man said. "We have plenty of victuals aboard. Even champagne, from that reception when we all arrived at the spa last night."

"The ball won't start until nine at least," Alice put in. "Loads of time. It's barely two o'clock now."

Daisy and William looked at one another. "I shall abide by your wishes," he said to her, light dancing in his eyes. "But I have no objections, either."

Daisy looked down at her best afternoon dress, which she had put on in anticipation of being visible by royalty, if not actually meeting them. "Will this do?"

"Admirably," William said. "I would marry you in a burlap sack. You know that."

"But we have no ring," she protested.

"The one you have is quite sufficient," Alice said dryly.

"Oh, my goodness." Daisy put her hands to her cheeks, which felt distinctly warm. "I hardly know what to do. Oh, dear. Oh, dear—"

"Davey, run to the boarding-house and fetch Elizabeth and Maylene," William said. "We cannot do anything about Jenny, I am sad to say, but at least we may secure two of the three."

"Are you really going to get married?" Davey asked, wide-eyed and poised to fly from the edge of his seat.

"We are," he said firmly. "We lift as soon as you get back. The Duke and Duchess's ball will be quite the second-rate affair compared to this."

2:20 p.m.

From this height, the archipelago lay in the straits like a handful of emeralds, casually scattered by a giant. The clear winter skies made the ocean as brilliant and deep a blue as any sapphire. Sir Ian locked the vanes so that *Swan* would make gentle circles of about a mile in diameter, then came forward to the main saloon to take his place before the largest viewing port, where nothing was visible for miles but sky and puffy clouds.

William, a snowdrop in his buttonhole, joined Sir Ian with Davey and Oscar at his side.

Freddie infinitely preferred the vast bowl of air to any cathedral. Here, surely, one was closest to God. She carried a nosegay of snowdrops tied up with a bit of ribbon Alice had unearthed from her trunk. Elizabeth, on her way to the ship, had hastily picked Daisy a bouquet of everything Montrose Birch's garden had to offer—the shy snowdrops, a few purple crocuses, and for a miracle, a sprig or two of golden yellow forsythia and one of rosy pink quince blossom. She may have arrived with her hat askew and her coat misbuttoned, but Beth certainly knew how to put a bouquet together.

A misty shape shimmered in a bar of sunlight. Clementine had followed Oscar aboard, and stood at the window as though she couldn't get enough of the view outside—nor of her son in his uniform within.

At a nod from the captain, Freddie heard her note in her head and began to sing. Not a hymn or a popular song suitable for nuptials, but one she had learned in Santa Fe, at the wedding of another happy bride.

> I have been lost upon the oceans
> I have seen stars fall in the seas
> I have sought you, Maraluna,
> For my home can only be
> In your heart, sweet Maraluna,
> In your arms that welcome me.

As she sang the song of the legendary queen, lost and then found, Freddie turned to gaze at her sister, walking in proudly on Papa's arm. She wore her afternoon dress and hat. No veil, no satin and tulle, no ring other than the Viceroy's ruby, which Oscar carried in his pocket for the ceremony. But there was no end to the love glowing in her eyes for her bridegroom as she paced toward him.

They were well matched, these two, though Freddie would never have imagined it when they'd met in Georgetown. Daisy had told her that poor William had just been thrown out of the doctor's surgery and on to the lawn when she had first happened upon him. But they had come through many a stormy sea since then. They were both brave, and resourceful, and filled with love for each other and those around them.

Daisy took her place on William's left, turned to kiss Papa, and on the final note of the song, handed her bouquet to Freddie with a kiss of thanks.

Sir Ian opened the prayer book at the place marked by a pressed flower that did not grow on this coast, Freddie was quite certain. She wondered if it had been in Alice's bouquet. Or if Alice, now dressed in a lovely silvery gown instead of her usual canvas pants and goggles, had even wanted a bouquet.

"Dearly beloved, we are gathered here today in the sight of God…"

Dear Davey stood bravely between William and Oscar, listening intently. He took the honor of groomsman much more seriously than any presentation to royalty. There had not been time yet to find him a suit of clothes, but Ian meant to slip over to Craigdarroch Castle and rummage through the boxes in the attic to see if something suitable might be found for this evening, at least.

"Daisy, will you have this man to be your husband—to live together in the covenant of marriage? Will you love him, comfort him, honor and keep him, in sickness and in health; and, forsaking all others, be faithful to him, as long as you both shall live?"

"I will," Daisy said softly.

William promised to do likewise, and they made their vows to each other. For richer and for poorer. The Viceroy's gold ingot would help them settle here in Victoria. Freddie was going to have to get used to the idea of being engaged to an aeronaut, and accept the fact that he must go where the RCAP needed him, whether that was here or Charlottetown or somewhere else. But she was determined that no matter where they found themselves after they were married, their home would always be here.

In sickness and in health. Freddie searched Oscar's face, noting that the bruises were more yellow today than green, and the swelling had gone down significantly.

To love and to cherish. She grew warm at the thought, and hastily lowered her lashes as Oscar realized she had been gazing at him moony-eyed all this time.

Distracted, it took him a moment to realize it was time to fish the ring out of his pocket. He handed the lovely ruby to William, who slid it once more on her sister's finger.

"Margrethe Amelia, I give you this ring as a symbol of my vow, and with all that I am, and all that I have, I love, honor, and cherish you."

Captain Sir Ian smiled as though this was the part he had been looking forward to. As they clasped hands, he said, "Now that Daisy and William have given themselves to each other by solemn vows, with the joining of hands and the giving and receiving of a ring, by the power vested in me by Her Majesty the Queen and the county of Somerset, I pronounce that they are husband and wife together. Those whom God has joined together let no one put asunder." The smile widened into a grin. "You may kiss your bride."

William took Daisy in his arms and kissed her soundly. Freddie would have clapped if her hands hadn't been full of delicate flowers, but Davey and their friends more than made up for it.

Daisy turned to collect her bouquet, tears of happiness welling in her eyes.

"Mrs Barnicott," Freddie murmured, and kissed her. "There. I said it first."

The saloon rang with congratulations and laughter, interrupted by the *pop!* of the champagne cork. "Beg pardon," Charlie said. "It got away from me."

"That one and many more," Alice said to him with a laugh. She raised her glass. "To the bride and groom."

They toasted William and Daisy, and the latter turned to her father. "To Papa, who braved any number of trials so he might walk me down the aisle."

With a broad smile, Papa toasted her, and then, mischief in his eyes, Freddie.

Captain Alice turned to Jake, who looked handsome in his navigator's khakis and yet still possessed an air of danger Freddie couldn't quite put her finger on. "This was my favorite wedding in the world," she said, "besides my own and Claire's."

"I'll drink to that," Jake said, and raised his glass. "Here's to the flock, wherever we find it, and long may it live."

And Daisy and William, Freddie and Oscar, the Professor and Mrs Birch, and even Davey with his thimble-sized share of bubbles, raised their glasses to the strangest and yet most wonderful toast Freddie had ever heard.

EPILOGUE

January 18, 1896

The Port Townsend Daily Leader
Morning edition

CARY CASTLE HOSTS DUKE AND DUCHESS OF CORNWALL
by Elizabeth Selkirk and Maylene Willamette

The highest echelons of society in Victoria, the Jewel of the Pacific, have lately been in a fever of anticipation to see who would be invited to the grand ball at Government House to welcome Their Royal Highnesses the Duke and Duchess of Cornwall to our fair coasts. The guest list was exclusive yet eclectic, in the opinion of these reporters. To those devotees of fashion, it may be confided that the Duchess was resplendent in silver shadow lace over midnight blue satin, wearing a tiara of diamonds topped by fourteen perfect pearls.

The Earl and Countess Dunsmuir arrived unexpectedly at

Craigdarroch Castle last evening, to take their rightful places as first after the royal couple among the glittering assembly. Sir Ian and Lady Hollys were in town for the occasion, Sir Ian being, of course, Lord John and Sir James Dunsmuir's cousin, enjoying the open doors of both Cary and Craigdarroch Castles. Another London notable present was Lady Langford of London and Surrey, on her second voyage after the sad passing of her husband, the fourth Baron Langford. But not all the guests enjoyed such titles and distinctions.

The guests were delighted to be introduced to the navigator of the Hollys vessel *Swan*, Jacob McTavish Fletcher who, along with his young half-brother David, had been working for the Royal Canadian Airborne Police in a clandestine capacity to bring about the end of the pirate scourge in the archipelago. As anyone who was in Victoria on Friday last may testify, they succeeded in spectacular fashion. Along with this military triumph in Her Majesty's name, young David rescued a young lady who had been in pirate captivity for five years, one Jennifer Anne Bodey, granddaughter of Dean and Mrs Bodey of the University. As one may imagine, their joy knows no bounds, as the late Corporal Allan Bodey and his wife were their only immediate family.

The Fletcher brothers were subsequently awarded the George Cross for, as Her Royal Highness said solemnly to Jake Fletcher as she pinned it to the breast of his uniform, "an act of the greatest heroism and most conspicuous courage in circumstances of extreme danger." Young David wore the silver cross on its blue ribbon—and Her Royal Highness's kiss —proudly for as late as he was permitted to stay up.

But the surprises in store for the evening were not over. Before dinner ended, His Royal Highness announced his plans to establish The Duke of Cornwall School of Applied and Engineering Physics, which will be led by its inaugural dean, Professor Rudolph Linden of Dresden and Edinburgh. Once a suitable building site is found, the school will operate in close cooperation with the University, giving its engineers and scientists an institution in which they can apply their knowledge of modern technology to the improvement and benefit of humanity.

It is greatly anticipated that such an institution, with the support of His Royal Highness himself, will make the Jewel of the Pacific shine even more brightly as we look into what must surely be a dazzling future.

THE END

AFTERWORD

Dear reader,

I hope you have enjoyed *The Professor Wore Prussian Blue*, and our adventures in the Magnificent Devices world. Daisy and Freddie's adventures conclude with this book, but there are many more to explore! You may have noticed the presence of Lady Langford in these pages. Watch for her intrepid adventures in solving mysteries in the Mysterious Devices series, beginning with a prequel, "The Air Affair," and then book one, *The Clockwork City*.

You might even go back to where it all began, with *Lady of Devices*, Magnificent Devices Book One, and learn exactly how Lady Claire Trevelyan met Davey's half brother Jake one dark, mysterious night (and yes, bombs were involved).

I invite you to visit shelleyadina.com to subscribe to my newsletter, browse my blog, and learn more about my books.

Welcome to the flock!

Warmly,

Shelley

ALSO BY SHELLEY ADINA

STEAMPUNK

The Magnificent Devices series

Lady of Devices

Her Own Devices

Magnificent Devices

Brilliant Devices

A Lady of Resources

A Lady of Spirit

A Lady of Integrity

A Gentleman of Means

Devices Brightly Shining (Christmas novella)

Fields of Air

Fields of Iron

Fields of Gold

Carrick House (novella)

Selwyn Place (novella)

Holly Cottage (novella)

Gwynn Place (novella)

Manor House Quartet

Acorn (novella)

Aster (novella)

Iris (novella)

Rosa (novella)

The Mysterious Devices series

The Bride Wore Constant White

The Dancer Wore Opera Rose

The Matchmaker Wore Mars Yellow

The Engineer Wore Venetian Red

The Judge Wore Lamp Black

The Professor Wore Prussian Blue

The Lady Georgia Brunel Mysteries

"The Air Affair" in Crime Wave: Women of a Certain Age

The Clockwork City

The Automaton Empress

The Engineer's Nemesis

The Wounded Airship

The Texican Tinkerer

The Aeronaut's Heir

The Regent's Devices series with R.E. Scott

The Emperor's Aeronaut

The Prince's Pilot

The Lady's Triumph

Shelley Adina is the author of more than 50 novels published by Harlequin, Warner, Hachette, and Moonshell Books, Inc., her own independent press. She writes steampunk adventure and mystery as Shelley Adina; as Charlotte Henry, writes classic Regency romance; and as Adina Senft, is the *USA Today* bestselling author of Amish women's fiction.

She holds a PhD in Creative Writing from Lancaster University in the UK. She won RWA's RITA Award® in 2005, and was a finalist in 2006. She appeared in the 2016 documentary film *Love Between the Covers*, is a popular speaker and convention panelist, and has been a guest on many podcasts, including Worldshapers and Realm of Books.

When she's not writing, Shelley is usually quilting, sewing historical costumes, or enjoying the garden with her flock of rescued chickens.

Shelley loves to talk with readers about books, chickens, and costuming!

Shelley loves to talk with readers about books, chickens, and costuming!
www.shelleyadina.com